Emily Thornton Charles

Lyrical Poems, Songs, Pastorals, Roundelays, War Poems, Madrigals

Emily Thornton Charles

Lyrical Poems, Songs, Pastorals, Roundelays, War Poems, Madrigals

ISBN/EAN: 9783744784795

Printed in Europe, USA, Canada, Australia, Japan

Cover: Foto ©Andreas Hilbeck / pixelio.de

More available books at **www.hansebooks.com**

LYRICAL POEMS,

SONGS,
PASTORALS,
ROUNDELAYS,
WAR POEMS,
MADRIGALS.

BY

EMILY THORNTON CHARLES,

(EMILY HAWTHORNE,)

AUTHOR OF "HAWTHORN BLOSSOMS."

Within my mind, in Nature's soil,
Some Flowers of Fancy grew;
Thoughts spring to verse as flowers to bloom—
Thus came this book for you.

WITH ILLUSTRATIONS.

SECOND EDITION.

PHILADELPHIA:
J. B. LIPPINCOTT COMPANY.
1887.

DEDICATION.

TO

LEWIS NATHANIEL AND MYLA CHARLES,

MY SON AND DAUGHTER,

WHO, FROM THEIR INFANCY, HAVE BEEN MY SOLACE AND CARE; WHOSE TENDER DEVOTION HAS
BEEN MY COMPENSATION IN HOURS OF SORROW AND ADVERSITY; WHOSE LOVE HAS BEEN
THE INSPIRATION TO GUIDE MY PEN TO LOVE'S EXPRESSION; TO LIFT MY MIND TO
BEAUTIFUL REALMS OF THOUGHT; TO WAKE IN DEPTHS OF FEELING, A
SYMPATHY FOR ALL WHO LOVE AND ALL WHO SUFFER,

THIS VOLUME

IS AFFECTIONATELY INSCRIBED BY THEIR MOTHER,

THE AUTHOR.

PREFACE.

My first volume, "Hawthorn Blossoms," was published in attractive form in 1876 by Messrs. Lippincott. It was all too hastily prepared for the press, and contained many crude specimens of verse, lacking in artistic finish.

It was put forth with fear and trembling on my part; but the critics magnanimously excused its faults and praised its beauties. The public received it with favor, partial friends patronized it, and the cluster of "Blossoms" proved not only successful but remunerative. The book has long been out of print, therefore a limited number of its poems are republished in these pages.

Some natures are developed, some mental traits or gifts are cultivated, only through the genial influence of encouragement, and while I concede that my simple songs of the heart were not deserving of the encomiums accorded them, yet the meed of praise has been to me a rare incentive to worthier efforts, a truer appreciation of art, and a more earnest endeavor to excel.

A few of these poems permit of the following brief explanation.

The "Souvenir to Longfellow" brought a response from him, in which he complimented also the poem "Unknown," and enclosed some autumn leaves accompanied by the well-known couplet, in his own clear chirography,—

> "The vine still clings to the mouldering wall,
> But at every gust the dead leaves fall."

This precious memento of the dead poet bears date November 5, 1881, and was probably one of the last souvenirs sent by his own hand. The engraving "Hope and Memory" was greatly admired, while yet in form of photograph, by Mr. Longfellow, as a beautiful group from real life.

"The Island Home" is situated in the Wabash River, at Logansport, Ind. It is the residence of Hon. H. P. Biddle, the poet-sage, the first literary mentor, sternest critic yet truest friend, of the author. Hon. Silas Wright, of Ohio, selected the Island Home as the theme and Shelley's "Cloud" as the style of versing, to test the author's facility for rhyming.

The address to "The Old State House" commemorates events and incidents in the history of that building, torn down in 1877, at Indianapolis, Ind. The poem, printed beneath a picture of the building, was placed by the late Vice-President, Mr. Hendricks, in the corner-stone of the new State House in 1880. To the picture and poem the following lines were added, which seem to apply nearly as well to these pages:

> When we, with years, have passed away,
>   This crypt shall then unfold
> Time's relics, here, without decay—
> The scenes that graced a former day,
>   Our memories of the old.

The impromptu, "At the Farm," was the last leaf introduced in this book. In March, 1886, it was written as a pleasantry in the body of a letter to the dear, genial poet to whom it is inscribed. In replying, he alluded in generous and charming manner to its style of his "Last Leaf" and the author's ready skill in versing.

To "Poetic License"—that "scapegoat" for the makers of faulty rhymes and limping verse—may be charged the liberty I have taken by the inscrip-

tion to several of our true *littérateurs* and distinguished countrymen, without
their knowledge or consent, of some few stanzas, regretting that the lines are
not more worthy their dedications. I would, indeed, that I were able to apos-
trophize in loftiest phrase and fitting tribute, all genuine poets in one.

The poet is a philanthropist, philosopher, and prophet. He understands
fully that the cold, practical world has neither inclination nor appreciation for
his flowing measures. He realizes that the same story he sings in verse may
be written in prose, and his purse grow plethoric thereby. He knows that the
utilitarian and scientist protest against the folly of verse-making as an employment; he hears the bustling man of business or the careful publisher aver
that "There is no money in poetry." Yet the poet sings away, and

> "Weaves his verses as the little birds
>   Build airy nests, because love bids him to."

His joy is to discover to himself and others, in written language, the beautiful thoughts that throng his mind, to feel that spark of inspiration that seems
to kindle his soul and sends a glow through his being, as his words flow in
rhyme and rhythm and measure that carry in their embrace gems of thought
that lie folded in beautiful simile, metaphor, or thrilling phrase. Under this
spell, the tear-drops of woe seem transformed to the pearls of wisdom, and he
feels that he has brought comfort to some heart longing for expression, and his
own heart is gladdened thereat.

Of the pleasure of versing, a distinguished poet once wrote me, "All that
the world can say to us, or of our poems, conveys not so much pleasure as we
have derived from their writing."

The poet is ever seeking, in the field of language, for the full expression of
something beautiful,—a thought perhaps that scarce can be defined,—when lo!
a flower of verse rises before his mental vision, and like a child elated with his
prize, he holds it up that others may see the thought that seemed so fair to
him, even before it bloomed in rhyme. Too frequently this feeling of exulta-
tion, though often followed by depression, is through misinterpretation termed
vanity, and the poor poet is made to suffer. The elusive character of thoughts
that seem to sing, and the difficulty of bringing them into the environment of
verse, is thus aptly described by a favorite poet:

> "So with thoughts my brain is peopled,
>   And they sing there all day long;
> But they will not fold their pinions
>   In the little cage of song."

A noted critic has said, "Every book should contain more of one's head
than one's heart." Yet every poet, and the majority of thinkers, will refute
the assertion, and perhaps agree with my THEORY OF POESY.

From the depth of the mine of human tenderness we obtain the hidden
wealth of emotion. Through the medium of the brain it is separated from
dross, and becomes beautiful thought; by patient labor this thought is coined
in appropriate words, and on these words is stamped the seal of love, the in-
signia of truth, and so the true lyric is formed.

I think it may be said that even wisdom is born in the heart though nurtured
in the mind.

I claim nothing for these songs except that, as they come from the heart,
they appeal to the heart, and perhaps endeavor to touch the vibrating chord
of sympathy that thrills the bosom of humanity, even though they express,—

> "Be it my woe or weal,
> Not what the head may know, but what the heart can feel."

                                                    THE AUTHOR.

CONTENTS.

Now charming Spring returns; soft breathes the balmy air
And welcomes blushing May, a scene most wondrous fair.

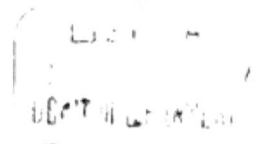

LYRICAL POEMS.

VACUNA'S REALM.

PROEM.

ENTHRONED on fleecy cloud Aurora lights the skies;
To usher in the morn, she bids the sun arise.
Behold the smiling dawn of loveliest month is born,
And nature's gladsome song floats on the wings of morn.
Now charming Spring returns; soft breathes the balmy air
And welcomes blushing May, a scene most wondrous fair.
Sol's marshalled rays swift dart through interstice of trees,
As cheerily they greet occiduous pungent breeze;
Or like setaceous spears, surround in brilliant guise,
As placed in line to guard sublunary paradise.
And Sol, with glow of joy, looks with lover's ardor o'er
The hills and grots and vales so fraught with mystic lore.

The mighty sun-god brings his retinue, each day
Of merry little beams, and sends them forth to play.
With flickering airy grace they rock upon the wave;
They throw their silver glints on strand where waters lave.
They kiss the billow's crest; chase shadows o'er the glade
And peep in sylvan nooks as they were half afraid.
Among the tree-top's leaves they play at hide-and-seek,
Or flying shadows catch in wayward fitful freak.
These sunbeams aureate but lightly go astray,
Such earnest triflers they, like children at their play.

Great mountain-laurels here uplift their shining sheen—
Their satin foliage of vivid glistening green.
Here sturdy giant oaks, the monarchs of the wood,
For many centuries have unmolested stood.
Low-bowed in vale beneath lithe willows kiss the brink
Of gurgling rivulets, where pretty creatures drink.

As infant that reclines on tender mother's breast
Sips from the snowy fount whereon it sinks to rest,
So gentle, soft-eyed kine o'er valley's vernal mead,
Like nurslings fair, recline on breast from which they feed,
While half suspended 'tween the sky and emerald sea
A soaring ship aloft in distance seems to be—
A white-winged messenger from far-off foreign shore
Draws near this peaceful port where perils reach no more.

In all the wide domain of mother-earth is not
Such soft salubrious clime, so fair a dwelling-spot;
Nor eyes have looked upon a peacefuller retreat,
Where sea and shore and vale and cloud and mountain greet.
Vacuna, rural sprite, here reigns in peace supreme
O'er all this verdurous realm, where houris sweetly dream.
Here purl the fountains clear, with lily-margined brink,
Whence Ganymede might bear the cup for gods to drink.

The leaping waterfall is laughing gleefully;
The brook with rippling song sets forth to find the sea;
The Austral wind responds to Zephyr's tender sigh,
And Aura whispers low to Iris fleeting by.
The drowsy bee invades the lily's fragrant bell,
Or lazily he drifts forth from his hermit cell
On nectariferous wings, of Hybla's sweets in quest,
To bear to Aristeus, to do the god's behest.

The shadows lightly sift through waving branch of trees;
Atremble are the leaves at touch of vagrant breeze,
And nature's myriad sounds in song of peace are heard;
Creation's mystic voice, through leaf and brook and bird—

The buzz of insect life, the slumbrous drone of bees,
The swish of ripening grain like wave of summer seas—
Unnumbered pipings pure in highest treble notes,
In subtle catches, roll, from tremulous feathered throats—
Pour forth in ecstasy, so clear each perfect trill
Affabrous pipes to mock, to scorn the Pan god's skill.
So blend ten thousand sounds, Vacuna's joy to share
In orisons that rise on palpitating air.

Fair Flora, lily-crowned, bedecks the lovely scene,
And calls her fairest subjects to beautify the green.
Her myriads of flowers, in fragrant, glorious bloom,
Freight all the sensuous air with incense of perfume—
Incense exhaled by dew, bright globes on flowers' crest,
That like the diamonds gleam upon a maiden's breast,
Or tiny blazing stars whose brilliant sparkles run
In evanescent rays to greet the rising sun.

Pomona, fruitful queen, with bounteous hand hath blessed,
And brings the luscious spheres by ardent suns caressed.
Here be the fruitage fair of tree and shrub and vine,
The orange, lime, and citron, the fig and nectarine.
A Naiad guards the fount near nitid esplanade,
Midst amaranthine bloom and arboretum shade.
Disporting here in glee, Aonian sisters nine
Pluck aromatic wealth from corymbiferous vine.

The Sun at close of day casts far his beaming eye
Ere he departs in glory to rule another sky ;
Then in the sea he dips the while his fervent rays
The ocean seems to crown with liquid golden blaze.
The light in mellow tints dissolves in ambient air,
Thus fading from the sight like scene surpassing fair.
Pale Luna's rays aslant entrancing dreams invite,
And weird enchantment lends to asteriferous night,
While through the woodlands fair a rover yet doth stray :
Sweet music on the air he wafts in roundelay :—

THE SWEETEST MUSIC.

Ah, many a day
Have I wandered away,
  Alone, to the forest glade,
Where all summer long
The wild bird's sweet song
  Was heard in the wild-wood shade.

With upturned face—
Where the alders grace
  The edge of the gurgling brook;
'Neath the elm-tree bough
I have bared my brow,
  And reclined in the sheltering nook.

Where the alders wave,
Near the brooklet's lave—
  The sky seemed a dome of blue,
While from leaves of trees,
Soft-stirred by the breeze,
  The sunshine was sifting through.

The ivy bringing
Its tendrils, clinging,
  A wreath-woven bower made;
Foliage twining
With grace, combining
  To deepen the welcome shade.

Where the blue-bird sang,
The robin's note rang—
  Cloud-tinted, the floating sky;
I long for that nook
And musical brook
  That ever goes flowing by,

Now murmuring sad,
Now joyous and glad,
   Now tenderly, soft, and low.
Sweeter music I've heard
Than the notes of a bird,
   In the brooklet's warbling flow.

Its sweet minstrelsy
Is freighted with glee
   Mellifluous, cheery, and strong,
And wisdom sincere
Who listens may hear
   Imparted by words of its song:—

THE SONG OF THE BROOK.

Run away! I'm at play.
I will catch you—I will catch you.
Run away.
Look out! Look out! Hear me shout,
See me play!
Jumping, leaping, dancing, creeping,

Laughing, babbling, singing, scrabbling
Funnily, as can be!
Tinkling, sighing, sprays aflying
Merrily, as you see.
Why so sad do you look?
That is bad; wear a smile;
Play awhile like the brook.
Do be glad;
Haste away; laugh and play.
Do as I do, do as I do—
Sing life through.
See me slide.   Only look,
Now I glide to this nook
Mossy lined.   You will find
Rhythmic music, potent logic
In the song of the brook.
Cascades leaping, never sleeping,
Courage keeping, sing and smile
With unceasing hope the while.
Move along, I am coming,
I am going, now I'm humming
Merry song.
Come again, come again;
I'm as busy as a bee—
Nearly dizzy.   Do you see
How I'm singing, changes ringing
Constantly.
Look at me now, look at me;
You shall see how, you shall see
Rocks I'm rifting, never drifting
Aimlessly.
I will find, some day,
Ne'er you mind, find a way
To the sea.
Look at me; would you win
Do as I do, do as I do;
Do begin;
Call it play, that is best.

By and by we shall rest,
You and I, by and by—
Rest for me in the sea,
From commotion ever free ;
Rest for thee, rest for thee,
On the ocean, life's eternity.

Then Zephyrus drew near; the flowers bloomed anew
And lifted their bright heads bespangled o'er with dew.
He called a vagrant muse to weave a dainty strain;
Of June, fair Flora's month, she sang, with sad refrain :—

IN JUNE.

The daisies are nodding o'er bending grass,
With bright eyes welcoming me as I pass,
As offering sweets, from a billowy knoll
The buttercup lifteth its golden bowl.
The feathery clouds float airily by
Flecking with silver the blue of the sky.

The mead seems a sea of green waves in the breeze,
Lithe branches are swaying of verdure-clad trees,
The clover-bloom perfumes the ambient air,
And, bride-like, all nature seems blushful and fair ;
The herds and flocks that browse on the green,
And ripening harvests, enhance the scene.

With lengthening shadows the days grow long,
And winged warblers their carols prolong ;
The wild bee rifles the flowers of the mead
Of mellifluous sweets, with true lover's greed ;
The murmuring brook sings merrily by ;
As I tremble with joy from my heart comes a sigh.

My thought too is stirred as by dalliant breeze,
My spirit is swayed like bough-bending trees ;
Like sweets in the clover the honey-bee sips
Emotions spring up to sweet words on my lips ;
My song rings out gladly like silvery bell,
Yet resounds on my heart like a funeral knell.

———

Now Orpheus appeared with emulant desire
And ardor new inspired.   He catches up his lyre ;
A low, sweet minor creeps across the silver strands
And e'en inanimates move forth at his commands,
For sky and sun and stars at evening's twilight hour
A glorious pageant seems by his supernal power :—

SUMMER TWILIGHT.

Daylight is dying, sunbeams are flying,
  Zephyrs are sighing, more pale is the rose ;
Sunset is beaming, starlight is gleaming,
  All nature seeming to smile in repose.

Sunset declining, God's law divining,
  Flying clouds lining with shimmering gold ;
Floating on high, night hastens the twilight,
  While through the sky bright cloudlets unfold.

Stars are besprinkling the sky ; their twinkling,
  Like chime-bells tinkling, charmeth each sense ;
Vanished the bright beam, come hath the light gleam,
  Stars to the night, seem a sweet recompense.

Ever the far bright gleam of the starlight
  Seems to debar night from gloomy unrest ;
Tenderly beaming, blessing in seeming,
  Floats through our dreaming a vision of rest.

Nature is stilling her children, willing,
   With rapture thrilling, and tend'rest care:
Daylight is dying; heavenward, sighing,
   Zephyrs are flying, as breathing our prayer.

Shadows are shifting, cloudlets are drifting,
   Night is uplifting her shadowy pall;
God's grace displaying, mandates obeying,
   Nature seems saying, "He reigns o'er all."

Fair Polyhymnia then, Vacuna bade attend,
To sing of Summer's scene, her eloquence to lend.
The lyric muse bent low, an inspiration caught,
And thus she set to words the music of her thought:—

THE SUMMER SOLSTICE.

Zephyrs are playing over the meadow,
   While light and shadow chequer the green;
Through leafy cover are sunbeams glancing,
   Brightly enhancing with beauty the scene.

'Neath branches swaying, the dew is laving,
   Emerald waving—setting of flowers;
As plea of lover with rapture thrills me,
   Emotion stills me—enthralls for hours.

O'er bending grasses, where dewdrops glisten,
   I lean and listen, while breath of spring
With incense laden, from field and flower,
   From sylvan bower, Heaven's praise doth sing.

O graceful masses! O lovely blending!
   O theme unending of mead and flower!
Builder of Aiden! my soul uplifted
   From shadows sifted, proclaims thy power.

In sheltering hover the birds are singing,
    The homage bringing of wordless voice;
Like harp-strings fairy, that zephyrs play on,
    In voiceless pæan, my thoughts rejoice.

From mead of clover, these thoughts upsoaring,
    To find their mooring, o'er perfumed bloom,
On pinions airy, heaven to inherit,
    Shall lift my spirit above the tomb.

From earth to sky was borne 'tranced thought of hearers then,
And Orpheus touched the lyre to wake its chords again,
While Ops, with modest mien, as Orphic-scenes dispersed,
An oral apologue, in pensive tones, rehearsed:—

THE INDIAN SUMMER.

Behold how time, with stealthy, noiseless pace,
Hath spanned another cycle-measured year,
And of all seasons, that most beautiful
Returns, the radiant Indian summer—
The breathing space, the solstice fair, between
The autumn's eve and winter's chilling morn.
It is as though the year were now restored
To spring-time loveliness and summer's guise
Of throbbing, glowing beauty, and had reached
The autumn's full fruition, to be wrapped
In snowy robe of winter, then to die.
This season, too, is like last parting gleam
Of sunlight as it bids farewell to earth
And glorifies the slow-departing day;
Or it is liken to a dying man:
Life's current now the fever has burned dry,
And, satiated, its ravages subside.
To consciousness he is restored.   His eyes
With lustrous brilliancy unwonted beam.

Unto his cheek, ersttime so pale and wan,
A semblance of returning health is given
By vivid hectic flush, false fleeting sign,
But none the less is he most surely doomed.

And thus the year is calmly beautiful
When near its close.   The stealthy Frost King then
Touches the foliage of tender green,
And gives a beauty hitherto unknown
To leafy vesture.   Lo! like Joseph's coat,
Of many colors, its hues are varied.
As autumn leaf is beautified by frost,
So does the touch of cold adversity
Develop beauty rare in flowers of thought;
And the mind ripens, as fruit is ripened
And mellowed by the chilling breath of frost,
By discipline of rude experience.

The year, having charmed the sight with festoons
Of graceful, twining vine, and vernal flower,
With meadow's sweetest bloom, and mossy nook—
Having unloosed the fetters that enchained
The bubbling brook and sent it on its way,
Gurgling, dancing, rippling in happy song—
Aye, the year, having panoplied the scene
With swaying vines fraught with purple clusters,
Having decorated the earth with sheaves
In shining masses of golden maize,
Laden the boughs with wealth of ripened fruit,
Is clad in many tints of richest hues,
And has attained the zenith of beauty
Ere it is folded in the snowy shroud,
To be borne beneath the funeral pall
Of icy-hearted winter to the tomb.

And what a fascination lingers e'er
In autumn woods!   Something, we know not what,

Some charmèd mystery, like vision fair,
Seems always to hover o'er and haunt them,
And hold our senses in willing thraldom.
Our thought even seems vague and shadowy,
And takes on more ethereal semblance,
And though pervaded with a sense of joy
That thrills our being, is tinged with sadness,
While we yield in silence to witchery
Of nature's smile, the spell of her magic wand.

The leaves are like bright-winged birds descending,
In variformed and variegated beauty,
To earth, in pendulous fluttering motion,
As the zephyr floating by lovingly
Caresses them and wafts them gently down.
The ripened nuts, bursting their cerements,
Fall thick and fast like globes of pelting hail,
As the breeze lifts the twigs whereto they cling
And sways the tree-top, that shall soon loom up
Stark and bare like corpse despoiled of covering.

Translucent and gold-glinted are the leaves,—
Slender oblong leaves of the hickory.
The kingly oak is clad in rich, dark crimson.
Touched with shaded purple and green satin.
The beech, by way of subduing contrast,
Wears a sober mantle of russet-brown;
And the leaves, beautiful leaves of the maple,
Are like the busy artist's palette, flecked
With all tints, from pale yellow, like the locks
Of a little child, to deepest orange
And amber; or are they not resplendent
In pink and rose, scarlet, and darkest red,
Even to maroon that borders on a brown,
As the tints reach their spiked and bevelled edges?

The soft green moss creeps up and warmly folds
Within its close embrace the crumbling trunk

Of the old worm-eaten, lightning-riven elm.
Above the moss is waving the ivy
In crimson masses of graceful foliage.
Even the gnarled old skeleton appears
Superbly beautiful, in phase of death.
The leaves, as we stoop low to gather them,
Rustle and sigh and moan, as they were wailing
A sad lament for the departing season.
Dissevered leaf-stems permeate the air
With pungent fragrance, as o'er all the scene
Is cast a hazy atmosphere like that
In ancient pictures seen, as covering
The coloring rich of autumn foliage.

Like a feathery cloud floating through space
Almost unconsciously our mental being
Drifts off into the realm of revery,
And the ideal fabric of the day-dream
Surrounds and folds us in ethereal mists.
Nature it seems, as pausing in her task,
Drew a deep full breath of inspiration,
And breathing forth again, wafted to us,
Like a lingering benediction pure,
The autumn solstice, the Indian summer.

In half-exultant voice was closed this long harangue.
Then Ops exhausted sank, o'ercome by tender pang.
Pomona, gentle one of countenance serene,
Pale Ops with love caressed, and led her from the scene.
Scarce time had intervened to hide them from the sight,
Vertumnus then appeared, his face with sorrow white.
He called Æolus down, and made a sad complain
That Eurus, eastern wind, had chilled the year with pain.
He bade Melpomene recite the dire mishap,
The dying of the year, and seasons, in his lap:—

THE DYING YEAR.

Chill and gloomy, bleak and drear,
Icy breath, the atmosphere;
  Never ending,
  Snow descending,
Dying is the poor old year.

Leafless trees with branches sere
Stand like sullen sentries here.
  Solemn towers
  Mark the hours
Of the swift departing year.

Listening watchers can but hear
Ghostly whispers sounding near;
  Voices hollow
  Seem to follow,
Sighing requiems for the year.

List, the wind doth howling veer;
Seemeth with sardonic jeer,
  Ne'er subsiding,
  E'er deriding,
Dying wailings of the year.

Murky skies more sad appear,
Weighted down with pity's tear.
  Winds are hurling,
  Snow-drifts swirling,
Round the fast expiring year.

Yea, the winds with antics queer,
Shrieking, through the curtains peer
  Seem as voicing
  Fierce rejoicing
At the dying of the year.

Tremblingly, as though with fear,
Floats the snow-flake, white and clear,
    And it glistens,
    As it listens
To the moanings of the year.

Farewell then, old friend, so dear;
Shroud him, snow-flake, make his bier.
    No set phrases
    Sound his praises;
Memory shrines the hallowed year.

Dead, the king! The king is here.
Death is birth! Bewail and cheer.
    Bells are tolling,—
    Anthems rolling,
Welcome to the coming year.

ALMA PERDIDA.*

In a tropical clime, when the day to repose
Floats softly as zephyrs' breath over the rose,
When the billows of ocean are kissed by the sun,
Thus nature proclaimeth a day's labor done ;
Piercing the twilight, come shrill, wild cries—
Thrilling the senses, the weird echoes rise—
A soul hath been lost! A soul hath been lost!
A vessel is wrecked, by life's breakers tossed.
Alma Perdida! A soul is lost!

---

* There is a bird in Peru to which the natives have given the beautiful name of
"Alma Perdida" (meaning the lost soul), whose cry is exceedingly melancholy. The
first note is shrill and long, and is followed by three more of the same length, but
which gradually deepen in tone. The Peruvians say it is bewailing the dead.

Say, heard ye that startling, that thrilling scream,
As infant's aroused by some horrible dream?
Like anguishing tremor of sorrow and pain
That stirreth the heart when we look on the slain?
'Tis a mourning-voiced bird, whose notes ever rise,
As the bird crying, sings, and singing, still cries,
Comes a cry from the soul, that is doomed to be lost,
A cry from the soul, whose path death hath crossed.
Alma Perdida! A soul is lost!

Heard ye that wailing, so yearnful and lone—
A shrill shriek dying in deepening tone?
It curdles the current of life in the breast
And rouses the senses to vague unrest.
A third time it rises, then mournfully dies,
Seeming to melt into tremulous sighs
For the soul that forever is lost,
For the sinking soul by the world engrossed.
Alma Perdida! A soul is lost!

Sad bird of Peru with the cloud-like wing,
And canst thou only a requiem sing?
Is this, then, thy mission? Art Heaven-sent
To symbolize woe in a woeful lament?
That a piercing scream from thy throat must rise,
A heart-rending shriek that in wailing dies,
For the soul that forever is lost?
Oh, spirit so fair and so pure thou wast!
Alma Perdida! A soul is lost!

Why should we rejoice when a soul is born,
A soul that may droop 'neath withering scorn;
With burdens of sin may downward be borne,
Its bright wings of hope all draggled and torn,
Till the spirit no more may soar to the skies?
So ever a wailing lament must rise
For the soul that is lost, ever lost, ˙
As flower transplanted is chilled by frost.
Alma Perdida! A soul is lost!

Oh, Alma Perdida, I know, I feel
The depth of anguish thy pipings reveal.
Thy lingering cry I never have heard,
Yet I grieve with thee, oh, sorrowful bird.
With thy wailing note my wail shall arise.
Our mournful dirges may pierce through the skies
And open the portals of Paradise.
I mourn with thee o'er the soul that is lost,
With prayerful moan for the life, tempest-tossed,
Alma Perdida!   A soul is lost!

Dost hover near me with shadowy wing,
The death of my spirit to mournfully sing?
Who knows if the longing and yearning soul
Shall soar like a bird to a heavenly goal?
Who but the Infinite, great All-wise,
Shall say if that spirit forever shall rise,
Or downward forever, forever be lost?
The oar-dip hath ceased ere the river is crossed!
Alma Perdida!   A soul is lost!

ROBERT BURNS.

WHERE Ayrshire's hills are lifted high,
As though to meet and kiss the sky;
Where cots in peaceful valleys lie,
      One glorious morn
Thou shouldst have sung, oh, bonnie Doon,
A merry, laughing, joyous tune;
Or flowed thy waves in rhythmic rune,
      When Burns was born?

Didst thou rejoice, oh, Scottish shire.
Did loftier grow thy towering spire,
When came to birth a soul of fire,
      A gifted son?

O'er Scotia lesser lights have shone;
None like to him the world has known,
He stands without a peer, alone—
    God made but one.

Could deep emotion's flowing tide
Have drawn him closely to your side,
And swept away your haughty pride,
    Oh, lordly clan,
His life was not with clouds o'ercast,
His heart not bared to meet the blast,
Like Scotia's crags, to storms that passed—
    A suffering man.

When noble lords in judgment sat
On peasant lad with brimless hat,
"A mon's a mon for a' that,"
    Bold Robbie sang.
The hills caught up the chorus brave,
Which answering cliffs resounding gave;
Never shall want be manhood's grave,
    The Echoes rang.

Of Scotland's hill, of Scotland's dell,
Of Highland lass he loved so well,
Nane sang sae sweet as sang himsel'
    The poet's song.
Emotion's fount with limpid flow
Touched every theme with nature's glow.
Would Scotland might the kindness show
    Denied too long!

His genius battled with its throes:
At length in majesty arose,
As wind-swayed pine the taller grows,
    His deathless fame.

A simple plough-boy's thrilling lays
Have stirred the world with joy's amaze;
Have crowned with laurel-wreath and bays
      The plough-boy's name.

Now scores of Winters intervene
Since oped his eyes to earthly scene,
Since first he saw the heather green
      In fragrance bloom;
Less by two score the Summers' hours;
As many Springs, have brought fresh flowers,
And cast where erst fell tears in showers
      Upon his tomb.

Now those who hold his memory dear
In hosts are gathering every year,
In every clime, afar or near,
      For Burns's sake.
To honor him who, sad, forlorn,
From morn till eve, from eve till morn,
Still sang inspired. The poet's born;
      Art cannot make.

His garb like birds that newly fledge;
His wit was sharp as sickle's edge,
Pointed and keen as thorny hedge
      Or feathered dart:
As Scotland's thistle—aye his pride—
Hides softest down 'neath rough outside.
So did his rough exterior hide
      The tenderest heart.

He sang of Scotia's sea-girt strand;
He sang of toil, and made it grand;
He sang to bless the peasant band,
      Pure joy to bring;

Of Caledonia far away,
Where tower those lofty peaks of gray,
The land caressed by ocean-spray,
         He loved to sing.

Had I a Sappho's tuneful lyre,
A Sappho's genius, quenchless fire,
I'd sound his praises sweeter, higher,
         In rhythmic lore.
I only with his laurels twine
A flower of verse from Freedom's shrine
To him who sang of "Auld Lang Syne"
         In days of yore.

Now Scotland's crags all bare and bleak,
Now Scotland's hills, from peak to peak,
Now countless tongues his praises speak,
         And graven urns.
As time shall pile the centuries high,
They'll form a column by and by
To him whose memory cannot die—
         Immortal Burns!

✓ OCEAN LEGEND.

AN IDYL OF THE OCCIDENT.

WITH Fancy—a realty never.
   I traversed the pebble-strewn strand,
Where the Ocean for ever and ever
   Embraces, caresses the land.

They formed for me scenes like Elysian,
   The sea and the sea-girded shore,
And I saw, as one sees in a vision,
   On the beach a volume of lore.

Though thought its still vigil is keeping,
  The volume I may not explore,
For its pages are sealed; I am weeping,
  And pacing the desolate shore.

But rising as dawn of the morning,
  Or mermaid out of the sea,
Or halo the sunset adorning,
  Came a semblance of beauty to me.

It was Nature in transcendent beauty,
  As fair as a glorious dream,
And I proffered allegiance and duty,
  And kneeled where she reigneth supreme.

I brought all the thoughts that came thronging,
  And sympathy sought in her breast,
With turbulent sobbing and longing,
  And she lulled me to quiet and rest.

Thus while at her feet I was kneeling
  She touched me with magical wand,
And I joyed with a rapture most thrilling—
  The key in my own heart was found.

She opened the heart in my being,
  And took from its casket the key—
Endowed me with new sense of seeing,
  And unlocked the treasure for me.

And leaning so smilingly o'er me,
  She bade me look lovingly 'round,
And the meaning of scenes spread before me
  Should all in the volume be found.

For the scenes were of Nature's portraying
  Wheresoever mine eyes did look,
And the lessons they taught, or were saying.
  I found them in Nature's own book.

Perhaps—it may be—I was dreaming
  And read not the mystical lore,
And that ever and only in seeming
  I conned Nature's legendry o'er.

I heed not who thus are divining;
  I listened to Nature's great law.
In her mandates my soul was enshrining
  True philosophy void of a flaw.

I claim not to be of the sages
  Who have studied the volume for years;
I have learned but a few of its pages,
  Albeit with sorrow and tears.

Each doubter may think what he pleases
  Of what on the beach I did see,
But I vow that the whispering breezes
  A love-story there told to me.

They said that the great grand Ocean
  A lover is, aged and gray;
That his heart ever throbs with emotion
  The whispering breezes say.

That the land is a mythical maiden
  Who reigneth a virginal queen,
Who with ermine in winter is laden—
  In summer with fair, vernal green;

That the Ocean is constant forever—
  The tale-telling whisperers say—
And for thousands of years he has never
  Neglected his duty to pay.

And they told me the hastening waves, that
  The sight in the distance may greet;
Are the myriads of Ocean's slaves, that
  He sendeth to fall at her feet.

Or perhaps, they come only to presage
  The arrival of Ocean, their king;
Or else a fond lover's sweet message
  To the maiden each moment they bring.

In billowy mirror she glances—
  She knoweth he soon will be there—
While the sunlight of heaven enhances
  Her beauty and makes her more fair.

Sometimes he is sighing and moaning
  Like a longing and yearning soul.
Sometimes he is inwardly groaning
  With feelings he cannot control.

Sometimes he so sadly is sobbing
  At her feet, like a weary child;
Or again, see the pulsating throbbing,
  As hearts throb with tumult so wild.

Sometimes he comes lovingly creeping,
  Like an infant to be caressed;
Or again, most joyously leaping,
  He clings to her neck and her breast.

And when he is tenderly sighing,
  And longing the bliss he would taste,
It is true there can be no denying
  He twineth his arm 'round her waist.

He loves with a love so enslaving,
  A devotion so loyal and sweet,
That he joys in quietly laving
  Her glistening sun-burnished feet.

Star-gems on his bosom are gleaming,
  And sun-rays make brilliant his crown;
His grandeur, a monarch's in seeming—
  He a monarch of wondrous renown.

The beautiful conch-shells are sounding
　　His coming that brooks no delay;
His billows catch up, lightly bounding,
　　And carry her image alway.

Battalions of waves are encroaching.
　　Tossing their white tasselled caps,
To herald the master approaching,
　　Whose love the fair maiden enwraps.

To do Ocean's bidding and pleasure,
　　From his storehouses deep, waves uplift
A wealth of his underworld treasure,
　　And bear to his sweetheart the gift.

Janthina, fair violet tinted—
　　Scalaria's turrets, so white—
The honey-combed corals indinted—
　　Pearl-shells tinged with amethyst light;

Most beautiful stones, trailing mosses,
　　Pearl and ruby and opaline gem—
Each wave, a swift courier, tosses
　　As fringe for her fair garment's hem.

She sits, like a beautiful maiden,
　　Clad in her verdure so fair,
Her presence an idyl of Aidenn,
　　Her brow fanned by ambient air.

So regal, in loveliness queenly,
　　So artless, so free from all guile;
She weaveth bright vesture, serenely,
　　And welcomes his coming, the while.

Her breasts are fair hill-sides of mosses;
　　Her neck, alabaster doth shine;
Her hair is the willow that tosses,
　　Her arms like the ivy entwine.

Her brow, sculptured height of the mountains;
　Fragrant pines, edge her radial crown;
Her laugh bubbles out of the fountains
　That leap her grand cliff-sides adown.

Her smile is the sunlight in gladness
　As she dippeth her face to his breast;
When clouds shade her brow as in sadness,
　His arms are her refuge of rest.

This story of loving devotion
　Was told, by the breezes, with glee,
As I stood by the shore of the Ocean
　And Nature was smiling on me.

I witnessed the lover-like meeting,
　And loitered on wide-spreading strand;
Old Ocean forever is greeting,
　Embracing and kissing the land.

As I drew me with reverence, nearer,
　To Nature's great heart-throb, I knew,
As my spirit-perceptions grew clearer,
　That the tale of the breezes was true.

The sunshine encalming the ocean,
　The rain-drops refresh g the land,
And feelings that thrill with emotion
　Are blessings from Nature's dear hand.

The breezes and zephyrs are voices
　That speak Nature's language sincere,
To the mortal who hears and rejoices,
　Having learned all her works to revere.

Nature's realm hath most wonderful glories
　For them who do lovingly look;
And lessons and legends and stories
　Embellish each page of her book.

The breezes impart them in whispers;
　The brooks babble fast as they flow;
The leaves and the zephyrs, fair lispers,
　Convey her sweet messages low.

And far the divinest of pleasures
　God giveth through Nature, so free,
And volumes of infinite treasures
　Her voices interpret for me.

Oh, Mortal, despairingly wailing,
　Creep closer, creep close to her heart;
For comfort and solace unfailing
　Her beautiful teachings impart.

THROUGH LIFE.

ENTERING life, we come fearfully
　Into the new and unknown;
Trembling and terrified, tearfully,
　Lifting life's burden alone,
Braving its danger more cheerfully
　When we the stronger have grown;

Still, like old Earth, so receivingly
　Taking the bad and the good,
Taking, nor choosing, believingly,
　Ever the best, as we could;
Sadly repenting, then grievingly
　Striving to do as we should.

Long may we wander suspectingly
　Ingrates whom passions enslave:

Scornfully, proudly, rejectingly,
   Serving the mercy God gave;
Nor look we to him who protectingly
   His arm forth stretches to save.

Thoughtlessly, carelessly, musingly,
   Playing at life's chequered game;
Ever the tally-sheet losingly
   Scoreth a list to our name;
Bravely our conscience accusingly
   Stirreth our senses to shame.

Looking to conscience inquiringly,
   Thoughtlessness seemeth a sin;
Working and striving untiringly,
   So must the battle begin.
Faith, hope, and love will inspiringly
   Teach us how life we may win.

May we our duty do darefully,
   Strengthening careworn, oppressed;
Threading our way ever carefully
   Through snares, to the home of the blest;
Hopefully, cheerfully, prayerfully,
   Finding in heaven a rest.

Striving with Sin, Sin enslavingly
   Holding us ever so fast;
Looking for mercy most cravingly
   Through the dark clouds sweeping past;
Tenderly, lovingly, savingly,
   Jesus redeemeth at last.

ECHO RIVER.

IN MAMMOTH CAVE, KENTUCKY.

SUNBEAMS never, mystic river,
Nor the moonbeams, o'er thee quiver;
Not the faintest starlight gleam
Shines above thee, sombre stream.
Night-enshrouded river Echo,
Mournful dirge so sadly slow,
Loudly clear or soft and low,
Singing as we gliding go—
O'er thy waters' silent flow
Comes the echo—" Lo."
See the shimmering shadows playing
Born of torchlights' fitful swaying,
Cast upon the cavern wall,
Cast o'er Echo River Hall,
    Hear the echo call,
Answering echo—" All."

And the boatman, standing grimly,
Throws a shadow weird, unseemly,
    On the rocky space,
    Strangely out of place,
As it were a net-work ghostly—" Lace."
Bright-winged birds have never flown
O'er thy waters dim and lone;
Shores of earth with flowers o'ergrown,
Mossy banks, lo, thou hast none;
Only walls of solid stone,
By the great Creator hewn,
    By His power alone
Bound thy waters—" Lone."

Wavering shadows weirdly falling,
Seem as spirits beckoning, calling,

Calling through the echo voices.
Strangely awed, our soul rejoices,
As 'twere voice from heaven calls us,
Heavenly majesty enthralls us.

Now from dome and wall surrounding,
'Gainst the massive rock resounding,
    Hear the echo
    Come and go.
Long we gaze in silent wonder.
We of earth thou'rt gliding under,
Through the rock reft wide asunder.

O'er thy watery depth rock-girten
Plays the flickering light uncertain ;
    See o'er dome and cavern hall
Tracery of mystic scroll,
" God's handwriting on the wall,"
    All His work, His—" All."

Hearken, now the voices singing,
All the echoes backward bringing,
As a grand triumphal ringing.
Every sense with rapture filling,
Like a thousand harpstrings thrilling,
Every breath to silence stilling ;
Joy divine is o'er me stealing,
    And a bliss profound
    Echo tells me—" Found,"
    In the echo sound.

Long the sweet refrain will linger,
As the trace of fairy finger,
Rising now in fuller volume,
Answering from each arch and column,
Joyous peals of music ringing,
As it were the angels singing.

Loud, resoundant, rising higher,
Melody of heavenly choir ;
   Is it this I hear ?
   Say, is heaven near ?
   This the spirit sphere ?
   List the echo—" Fear !"

To my mind this truth is plain :
Know I now by this refrain
Words that die will live again.
And the grand resurgence rolling,
All my inner soul controlling,
   Echoes ever
   O'er the river,
Stirs this thought within my brain,
As a loudly-echoing strain,
Words may die yet live again.

Fairy river, gliding, going,
Through the cavern, winding, flowing,
To the wondrous realm beyond,
Here my thirsting soul hath found
Peace my longing soul had wanted,
Quelled are doubts of spirit haunted.
Thou hast taught me more than sages
By thy rocky clefts of ages,
Taught me more than storied pages ;
Led me to the opening portal,
Proved the soul is e'er immortal ;
Brought of knowledge mighty store,
Hidden in mysterious lore.

Echoing thoughts my brain are stirring,
Ever to my mind recurring,
Evermore this truth averring ;
Thou hast taught by sure refrain,
Echoing dying words so plain,
I shall die, yet live again ;
Dying be my—" Gain."

THE OLD STATE HOUSE.

[A REMINISCENCE.]

OLD stately hall, thy day of grandeur's past;
Outlived, like grim old age, thy usefulness.
Joined now to the destroying hand of time
Is that of lordly man to lay thee low.
Thy columns grand—like those of Parthenon,
The pride of ancient Greece—are doomed to fall.
Their solemn thud, resounding on my heart,
Wake mournful, saddening echoes of the past,
And rouse my thought to pleasing recollection.

A romping child I gambolled o'er thy sward,
And gazed with wonder on thy massive form.
E'en then my bosom thrilled with statesman's pride.
I stood and looked upon thy pillars grand,
Surmounted by thy shining, silv'ry dome,
O'er which our flag was floating on the breeze,
Nor deemed in all the realm thou hadst a peer.
How oft with throng of little ones I've played
About thy mouldering walls at hide-and-seek;
With reckless, thoughtless tread and clinging hands
Skimmed round the columns that enribbed thy side,
And stood an instant in each recess hid,
A breathing statue; or with headlong haste
Went tumbling to the ground; rose quickly up,
And to it again, as 'twere the menaced danger
Made our footsteps eager. Ersttimes we dared,
Yet bolder grown, within thy sounding hall,
Like tunnelled bridge, to tread; followed thy winding stair;
At lofty height we reached thy windowed dome,
And quickly ran from this outlook to that,
To see what vast extent comprised our world.

By daring urged, our brother scaled thy roof,
And stood like one who had achieved renown.
How oft when glorious Independence Day
Came round marched in thy grounds a youthful host
From all the Sabbath-schools—the girls white-robed,
With flowing sash of blue and flowery wreath—
White pantalooned, straw-hatted were the boys.
The long procession, headed by our chief,
Snow-haired and sunny-faced, who charged us oft,
When all were seated, to pay attention
To the speaker's words who should address us.
A thousand childish voices rose in song,
Borne upward on the air; then followed prayer,
And then the Declaration grand was read,
The which, I now declare, seemed overlong.
Then, best of all, there came the feast of cakes,
And snowy rolls were passed to every child,
And tin cup bright, with liquid crystal filled,
Refreshing as the falling dews of heaven
Refresh the thirsting earth, to us.
Then came release and careless glee, until
The long, long summer's day drew near its close.

Thy floor has echoed to the martial tread,
In later years, of brave and stalwart men,
Who, loyal, answered to their country's call.
Here sat the chief executive of state,
Our great war Governor,* issuing commands,
A leader born.   Here, too, he should have lain
In death's repose.   Within thy halls that voice,
Whose clarion notes are stilled in icy death,
Hath thrilled with patriotic fire the multitude,
And roused the soldier's pride and valor.
Here he had served his State and country best,
Drew most upon the people's gratitude,
And won renown by deeds that e'er shall live.

---

* Oliver P. Morton, of Indiana.

In memory's glass once more I see thy walls,
All clad in black, thy halls in mourning shrouded,
While still the heavy-laden clouds o'erhead
Drop sympathetic tears with those who weep.
Within thy central aisle I seem to see
The piled sarcophagus enwreathed with flowers.
The dais raised, the velvet funeral pall
On which the martyr patriot, Lincoln, lay.
The mournful throng, the grieving multitude,
That in the mud and rain stood patient, waiting,
Or that, by twos and twos, still filed along,
To gaze once more through falling tears upon
The nation's murdered chieftain. There he lay,
Like one " who wraps the drapery of his couch
About him, and lies down to pleasant dreams,"
Who all unconsciously is borne along,
Mourned and wept over, eulogized and loved,
Yet, undisturbed, sleeps on in rest eternal.

Within thy ancient walls the learnèd pundits
Of our State, with dignity assembled ;
The wigs of wisdom met in secret conclave.
There came the orator with loud debate,
And able lawyers pleading for the law.
There stood the granger, here the city gent,
And argued which was best, the this, or that ;
This bill, one knew, expressed the people's will ;
Another thought the opposite was true ;
Each one being bent to do the thing he thought
Best pleasing to his own constituents.
And thus they builded up cross-purposes,
'Neath which the general good was overlooked.
Throughout the world each party faction seeks
But to complete its own aggrandizement ;
Each creed looks only to its own upbuilding,
Few nobly seeking e'er unselfishly,
The public weal, to evangelize the world.

But thou art now a mass of falling ruins
Soon thy loved form will disappear from view,
Yet linger in the mind, freighted with thoughts
And hosts of recollections; then I hear
Echoes of youthful laughter, careless glee—
In memory's magic mirror contemplate
Pictures of years gone by; when memory fails,
Then thou shalt live in history, as one
Whose death marks eras of events and deeds.

DAISIES AND BUTTERCUPS.

Daisies and buttercups, lovely are ye,
Daisies and buttercups, seeming to be
Drifting and swaying on meadowy sea,
Nodding and bending and bowing to me,
Ye wave o'er the billowy, flowery lea.

A golden cup and a porcelain plate,
With gold embossed—I shall banquet in state
From fairy flowers that zephyrs undate;
I will dine with love, I will banish hate,
And the nectar of gods my mind shall elate.

This flowery censer with gold enwrought,
With costliest, rarest of dainties is fraught,
And laden with clusters of beautiful thought;
I gather their sweets which nepenthe hath brought,
For which my sad mind had long languishing sought.

As the shimmering waves around me roll,
I partake, as I rest on a billowy knoll,
Of feast of reason and flow of soul;
'Tis a mystic chalice, thy golden bowl,
And I quaff from its hollow no meagre dole.

As I lift the goblet filled to the brink,
Encorralled about with a green leafy link,
The bright cups jingle, and seem to clink
With a joyous ring as I stoop to drink,
And, wrapped in day-dreams, I blissfully sink;

And a purer thrill of pleasure is mine
Than any that lurks in the sparkling wine
From the purple wealth of the leafy vine.
This richest surfeit can never be thine
Till thou drinkest to love and kneel at love's shrine.

There's a mystical spell in the goblet, I ween,
That giveth new beauty to velvety green,
That addeth a glory to shimmering sheen
Cast over the waves gliding through the ravine,
For a golden halo encircles each scene.

There's a cloud-capped mountain that loometh high
Through the ethery blue of a tropical sky,
Where the kisses of muses float airily by,
Borne on the breath of a zephyr's soft sigh,
And I yearningly longed to its summit to fly.

Far up, where the clouds and the mountain greet,
There's a fountain pure and as nectarine sweet,
Whose waters e'er flow with a rhythmical beat;
Here it is that the naiads and muses meet,
And quaff from this fountain of bliss complete.

That I never could reach this fountain I knew,
Yet my longing took wings and heavenward flew,
Through the vasty depth of empyrean blue,
To the waters which, tasted, none ever may rue,
Then whispered my thought to Thalia so true.

As I drink to love, and love drinketh to me,
From the flower-cup sweets, as culls honey the bee;

O'er thy swaying bloom, comes, like sigh o'er the sea,
The murmur of muses; Thalia gave me
To sip from the fountain of Castaly.

For the gentle muse, with a sympathy true,
Leaning over the marge where fair flowers grew,
Caught the drips from the fountain and upward threw;
As she flung them aloft, they descended in *dew*,
And fell in the cup, I am drinking to you.

Still over the meadow the zephyrs that blow
Are whispering ever in breathings low,
That thrill me with pleasure. With joy I glow,
And an ecstatic thrill through my being doth flow,
Yet the source of my pleasure I scarcely may know.

Oh, daisies and buttercups! never I see
Thy swaying bloom but there cometh to me
Fancies recurring and fancies that flee,
And I yearningly long for quiet with thee:
From the world and its tumult I long to be free.

THE SEA-ANEMONE.

In the vasty deep of the sun-kissed sea
Thou dwellest, oh, lovely Anemone!
Tinted like shell of the coralline cave,
Gracefully swaying to meet the blue wave;
Orphean strains would I breathe over thee,
Blooming in loveliness under the sea.

Under the glimmer of silvery sheen,
In blushful beauty thou'rt lying unseen;
Gliding so slowly from sea-shell to rock,
Lightly withstanding the rude tempest-shock;

Safe sheltered from storms; 'twere joy thus to be
Harbored from harm, 'neath the waves of the sea.

Would you had language—to me you might tell
Of the sea-green caves where the mermaids dwell;
Of the siren's song, where, at midnight hour,
You brighten the walls of the sea-nymph's bower;
Where storms never sweep o'er the tranquil lea,
Down in the depths of the fathomless sea.

Is the hermit-crab bold still wrestling well,
Despoiling his brother of loftier shell?
Does the sea-horse rear its beautiful head?
Does the skate-fish soar like a kite outspread?
A billow the dolphin still seem to be,
Tumbling and rolling o'er mountains of sea?

Do the fish in shoals seek the sea-moss glade?
The sea-ravens bask in the silent shade?
Does the moon-fish lighten the glade at night?
Or sunfish bring it a radiance bright?
Was ever another as fair as thee,
Dwelling far down 'neath the billowy sea?

Is the conch-shell sounding the ocean's roar?
Lifteth its pinions, the gurnard, to soar?
Does the turtle sleep?   The cockle-shell float?
The nautilus sail in fairy-like boat?
Unfettered are all, untrammelled, and free
In soundless depths of the turbulent sea?

Does the seal uplift its innocent eyes
In childlike beauty of trust and surprise?
And what is janthina's vocation, pray tell,
Of beautiful, violet-tinted shell?
Oh, would you might whisper a story to me
And tell what they're doing down deep in the sea.

Do the cuttle-fish cling to ships till they sink,
And blacken the water around them with ink?
The devil-fish downward forever draw
The small fry into his terrible maw?
Do they find too late that they cannot flee
From Satan who dwells in depths of the sea?

Who reared scalaria's turreted height,
With steps leading upward so pure and white?
What gave thee thy colors, from sunny glint
To brightest and deepest cornelian tint?
Do tell me, oh, tell me, Anemone.
Tell me of all that abide in the sea.

Does the whale still hover like cloud o'erhead,
Where cyclops are tinting the ocean red?
Is the lobster hiding in silvery sand?
The scallop a pilgrim to far Holy Land?
Oh, can you not tell me, Anemone!
What are they all doing under the sea?

Does the sea-lion toss his glistening mane?
Does the shark gloat over his victims, slain?
Are corals at work on the pink-white strand,
Building a palace for Neptune, so grand,
Where the Sea-God may rest, if rest there be,
'Neath the surging tide of unresting sea?

What gave to thy brother the form of a star?
Reflected light of that orb from afar?
Though silent and still—for you have no voice—
Your God-given mission makes me rejoice,
For He is speaking through you unto me,
From far away depths of the mystical sea.

He teaches that beauty in nature dwells
From heavenly dome to cavernous cells;

That the world He hath made is fair and bright,
If with loving senses we view it aright.
A zoophyte fair, and a flower you be,
Waving and blooming on rocks of the sea.

Like a human flow'ret so too am I,
Swayed rudely by breezes that pass me by;
Shaken like reed by the storms of life;
Tossed by the billows of tumult and strife;
Seeking a haven, a sheltering lee;
Finding no rest on life's pulsating sea.

Yet could I dwell under the trackless wave
And frequent the haunt of the coral-cave,
I would scatter the spray of the salt-sea foam
And down, down deep in the ocean would roam.
I would meet you and greet you, Anemone;
Together we'd traverse the vast blue sea.

I would list to the tale of the sounding shell,
Hear nature's own song in its surge and swell.
On the shifting sands I would seek pearl gems
And string them on sea-moss for diadems.
Fair Nature would teach me, Anemone,
The secrets now hid in mysterious sea.

Aye, Nature would teach me the mystical lore
Of the deep-sea world, realms I would explore.
I would heed her lessons, interpret her signs,
And speak for ye all as my heart divines
In tones that are thrilling in sympathy,
Oh, wonderful creatures in wonderful sea!

MEMENTO MORI.

Ah, who shall tell the tears I've shed,
The storms of sorrow I am breasting,
Or weave in verse the mournful story!
Now Love once warm and true is dead,
That folded in my heart was resting.
Ah! sadly mournful, plaintive story
Is told in this—*Memento mori.*

For happiness, too, fled away,
And evermore was unreturning;
It blazed awhile in golden glory;
Like meteor-flash 'twas gone one day,
As candle low in socket burning.
'Twas but a parting gleam of glory.
I moaning sigh—*Memento mori.*

Alas! I mourn that joys have fled
With happy days now gone forever,
For death stalks forth all grim and gory.
The friends I loved—they, too, are dead,
Ties sundered death alone could sever
With sickle keen and sharp and gory.
I grieve therefor—*Memento mori.*

Yet Hope I claim she is my own,
Henceforward by my side remaining.
Then let me weave a brighter story;
Hope lingers still—I'm not alone—
Why vainly should I be complaining,
And sadly wail the direful story,
With thrilling cry—*Memento mori?*

And Faith is mine. I do not dream;
The darkest clouds are shadows shifting;

The sun still shines in undimmed glory,
And I rejoice in Faith supreme—
Faith evermore my soul uplifting,
That sees through clouds omniscient glory.
Then wherefore weep?—*Memento mori.*

And so erstwhile I thought that Love
Was dead, but Love was only sleeping.
Love thrills me now with mystic story,
And whispers that, in realms above,
Love's angels watch o'er me are keeping.
I do believe the wondrous story.
Why should I grieve?—*Memento mori.*

Cease, then, my soul—why thus complain?
Though ofttimes sad, be hopeless never;
But lift in praise a song of glory.
Three heaven-sent messengers remain—
Faith, Hope, and Love shall live forever.
God reigns o'er all—be His the glory.
I sing no more—*Memento mori.*

CLEOPATRA.

Cleopatra, glorious name!
In dreams to me a vision came,
And bade me sound again thy fame,
And weave anew thy glowing story,
"L'Orient's" pride, old Egypt's glory;
Yea, pictures on the wall of time
My dreams of thee, and thy fair clime.

All radiant as a bright-winged bird,
In dreams thy perfumed breath hath stirred
My sleeping heart, and I have heard

Thy silvery tones, like music swaying,
In rippling waves of laughter playing.
I seem to see a form divine;
Ah, peerless one, that form is thine.

Thus I might warble sweetest lays,
With poet's mystic power to raise
The thrilling song; thy beauty praise,
While Greece and Egypt, both combining,
Their names with thine are intertwining,
Uniting thus to form, through thee,
One blazoned page in history.

More beauteous one was never seen
Than Egypt's Circe, Siren, Queen;
Enchantress bright of royal mien—
Through royal weakness, lovers sighing,
Where squadrons conquered, hosts lay dying.
Unmoved by loyal Antony's fate
Before thee fell the Cæsar great.

Thy standard high, like flag unfurled,
Thy beauty conquered all the world;
Thy passion-words were missiles hurled;
Or changed to loving accents flowing,
They fell from lips like rubies glowing,
While nameless charms combined as well
To strengthen thy alluring spell.

Thou hadst a queenly, haughty pride,
A beauty almost deified;
To win thy love kings would have died.
Thy life was spent in wanton whiling,
From duty's path thy slaves beguiling,
Swaying the mind with studied art,
Moving to sensuous love the heart.

And yet, in all thy perfect face,
Thy lovely guise, thy form of grace,
Unselfish goodness found no place.

In wayward thoughts and deeds delighting,
The fairest lives forever blighting,
Thy words, thy grace, thy lustrous eyes,
Were weapons used to tyrannize.

Looking with retrospective sight,
I see thee reign through beauty's might,
Nor use thy power to wield it right;
Laughing in glee at lover's raving,
With pleasure's chains the throng enslaving.
Too true, too true, the comment sad,
For such as thou a world went mad.

THE CHILD OF GENIUS.

INSCRIBED TO R. H. S.

THEY say that o'er the poet's brow
  Genius hath cast a glorious light;
That when 'neath sorrows he would bow,
  Dispels the clouds with radiance bright.

Who would the child of genius be,
  To suffer and grow wisely sad—
With prescient eye earth's wrongs to see,
  Earth's pleasures quaff, yet ne'er be glad?

In brooding sadness, day by day,
  To dream of peace that ne'er is known;
To weep, alas! to hope and pray
  As one who would for guilt atone?

To see the world in waking dream
  Moved by the sordid, ruled by wrong;
Where fraud and guile the fairest seem
  And stir the thought to saddest song?

Man lifted by ill-gotten gain,
  Spurning in dust his brother man,
Whose life hath been one breath of pain
  Since first that span of life began?

Perched high on earth's triumphal car
  With pomp and show the proud are borne;
Yet by the humblest thousands are
  The battle-scars of life well worn.

Behold a brother's care and pain,
  The gilded snare, the trickster's play,
Nor wonder that a sad refrain
  Haunteth the poet's roundelay.

Thus earthly wrong doth genius see;
  For this doth ever genius mourn.
Ah, then in pity who would be
  A child of heavenly genius born?

A child to grieve, and moan, and sigh
  For things another never may;
To come to birth with wailing cry
  A *hundred* years before its day.

THE KISS AND TEAR.

If untold bliss
Lurks in a kiss,
There's something more endears;
More precious far
Than kisses, are
The welling, heart-felt tears.

Who nectar sips
From dewy lips,
Would find a fount more dear;
If they who'd snatch
A kiss, would catch
The dearer, falling tear.

Love-light we prize
Beams in the eyes,
The sense of joy most dear;
Love's purest glance,
Tear-drops enhance,
The silent, unchecked tear.

The memory
Of sympathy
Shines through the mist of years;
As light that dies
In sunset skies
Shines through the rain-drop tears.

When I am glad,
Or when I'm sad,
I'll bring thee what endears;
It lies in this,
The chastened bliss,
The tenderness of tears.

'Twere sweet to rest
On faithful breast,
And cast aside all fears;
There bring the bliss
Of love's pure kiss,
There find relief in tears.

When stilly death,
With chilly breath,
Shall quell heart-throbs and fears;

Then o'er my brow—
Oh, why not now?—
Thou'lt shed affection's tears.

And shouldst thou miss
The loving kiss,
That memory still reveres;
Then lingers yet
This fond regret,
I might have caught her tears!

RACHEL.

FOLD my garments of sackcloth about me;
The ashes of a dead hope are upon my head;
The bitterness of Dead Sea fruit is on my lips;
An aching pang corrodes and rends my bosom—
Cursed and suffering with a fierce unrest;
Pitiable, pitiable object that I am!

Hear ye not, oh, Lord! the cry of my wounded heart,
Tugging at the cords that hold it in my breast?
Feel ye not its wild, impatient yearning?
Its crazed anguish, throbbing, struggling
To burst the cerements that bind it
In earthly clay, though but to fall,
A quivering, bleeding mass?

Torture! torture! and wilful raving—
Oh, my children! life of my life; soul of my soul;
Where are ye?   Gone forever!
Mine; ye were all mine; who hath dared
Sever the tie that bound ye to me?
Ye blessed ones, my babes,
Speak to me, beloved; answer
The call of my heart, or I die!

The sweetest music hath no sound
Like to your rippling laughter;
The fairest flower is still less fair than ye;
The brightest star that gemmed the firmament
Grew dim beside the lustre of your eyes;
While your hastening footsteps wakened
Joyous echoes on my listening heart.

Now! now! ye answer not my pleading;
Respond no more to my burning kisses;
Like broken lilies, pale ye are;
Your arms cling not so lovingly
About my neck. Ye spring no more,
With buoyant step, to meet me;
Dimmed is the life-light of your eyes;
Ye know me not—ye answer not.
Cold and dead ye lie—cold and dead;
Woe is me! dead! dead! I too will die!
Bury me with my darlings;
Fold my cold arms round their loved forms;
Clasp in mine own their dimpled hands;
So! now bury us, bury us deep!
*   *   *   *   *   *   *   *

Horror! horror! my heart will not die;
It rends and tears my bosom,
But alas! it will not, cannot die.
Take it away, oh, Father,
Smother its tumultuous throbbing;
Then may I sleep, sleep with my babes.
Hold! ye shall not wrest them from me;
They are mine, I say, mine own;
Though ye rend me in pieces
I will not yield them; they are mine! mine!

Mine! Hear the shouts of derision,
Scoffs and sneers at impotent rage!
None can fathom a mother's anguish;
Her heart despoiled of its jewels,

None but a mother bereaved,
A mother's sorrow may know;
None but the eye all-seeing
Can measure the depth of her woe
Crazed, rebellious, and raving—
Wailing for comfort and rest.

A LESSON IN BOTANY.

VIOLET, sweet violet,
I love you as I love my pet.
Lifting so modestly thy pure face
Decking the bank with thine azurey grace.
Let me see—
One, two, three,
Four, five—ever five leaves;
Five is the number that never deceives.
What care I for your family?
What did you say?
Botany?
Fling it in Botany Bay.

Daisies, daisies,
Scattered in endless mazes
Over the meadows, under the hedges,
Not in the path, but close to its edges;
As stars gem the blue of the sky with their sheen,
Ye gem and besprinkle the velvety green.
What care I for your pedigree?
Pistils or stamens, how many there be!
What did you say?
Botany?
Fling it in Botany Bay.

Buttercup!
Hey, johnny-jump-up!
Johnny will tell if I pull you apart—
If I pick you to pieces and tear out your heart,
Johnny will tell,
I know him well,
So keep your heart in its golden bell.
What care I how rich it be!
I love you, and that sufficeth me.
What did you say?
Botany?
Fling it in Botany Bay.

Forget-me-not!
I love the spot
Where grows the fairy forget-me-not.
How like to a star
Its pale blossoms are!
And its bonny bright eyes I love to see.
What care I how many there be?
What did you say?
Botany?
Fling it in Botany Bay.

Mignonette!
I'll never forget
Thy fragrance; it lingers about me yet.
Delicate blossom,
Rest on my bosom,
Shed a sweet incense, when dying, o'er me—
When my vision no more thy flower shall see.
What did you say?
Botany?
Fling it in Botany Bay.

Lily so fair!
Purity's there.
You have beautiful raiment and never a care.

Oh, would I might be
As lovely as thee,
And have never a thought about "nothing to wear!"
I'd belong to your "tribe," whatever it be.
What did you say?
Botany?
Fling it in Botany Bay.

And cowslips!
Dewy lips,
Thy name recalls bright childhood scenes;
For thy blossoms I look,
In the mead, by the brook,
Through the vista of time that intervenes;
Again I chase the wingèd hours,
And gather thy yellow unfolding flowers,
Golden boats all afloat on a green leafy sea.
What did you say?
Botany?
Fling it in Botany Bay.

Bluebells, bluebells,
What have you hid in your airy cells?
Azure of heaven,
Dewdrops of even—
Whisper, bluebells, whisper to me;
I only know how fair you be,
Without a thought of your family.
What did you say?
Botany?
Fling it in Botany Bay.

Fair budding rose—
I may not close
Without a tribute in verse to thee.
"First love!"
May it prove

Source of joy like flowers to me,
Whatever their names or their family.
What did you say?
Botany?
Fling it in Botany Bay.

Orange blossom!
Adorning the bosom,
Or twined in the curl of a fair lady's hair;
Ah, sometimes you be
But a mockery;
Her lips may be false, though her brow seem so fair—
Then so many heart-aches you blossoms are.
Joy, trouble, or care is your progeny,
A various, wonderful family.
What did you say?
Botany?
Fling it in Botany Bay.

Pansies are fraught
With beautiful thought;
Bright thought and golden, and brilliant in hue;
Give me the blue one, that is the true one.
I'll have nothing to do—
Pansy, would you?—
With "genus," or "classes," or "family."
You bring a thought, a dear thought to me.
A thought, did I say?
For my botany?
No! fling it in Botany Bay.

Poppy—nepenthe—
Tell me who sent thee
To lull me to sleep o'er my botany?
So drowsy am I—
I cannot tell why—

Nor how—many—stamens—or—poppies I see;
I cannot remember how many there be.
What did you say?
Botany?
Go fling it in Botany Bay.

A SPRAY OF FLOWERS I BRING THEE.

A SPRAY of flowers I bring thee, friendship's token,
  Though many wither 'neath the noontide sun,
Bedewed with tears from clouds of grief unspoken,
  Hoping that memory's vase will nourish one.

My path was rough—few flowers grew by the way—
  But finding on a jagged, rocky slope,
There gathered I this simple hawthorn spray;
  And bring to thee a flower that breathes of hope.

Behold, the morn beyond the night is breaking
  That bringeth forth a brighter, fairer day;
And o'er the earth the glorious sun, awaking,
  Riseth, and sends the sunbeams out to play.

Thus glorious hope doth rise within the bosom,
  Beyond the gloomy night of grief and care;
So may these flowers mature in perfect blossom,
  Bright hopes spring up, choking the weed, despair.

Hope's buds are sometimes but the opening flowers,
  That, ere they blossom, crushed and blasted lie;
So buds of thought, beguiling weary hours,
  May die, and yet their mission ne'er can die.

What though on earth our hopes ne'er find fruition,
    And blossoms fade and reach a sere decay;
These flowers have still fulfilled their truest mission,
    And sometimes driven doubt and fear away.

And, though my garland has no beauteous blossom,
    No budding thought that sprang to perfect bloom,
Bury it with me, folded on my bosom;
    My flowers of hope will thrive beyond the tomb.

Receive my flowers; they have no shine of splendor,
    Yet costlier tribute ne'er was brought to king;
The price was love, grief, pain, and memories tender;
    The gift, though small, was all I had to bring.

RETRIBUTION.

I HEAR the throb through the murmur of song
Of a heart low bowed 'neath burden of wrong,
And a thrill responsive is stirring my breast.
Take comfort; who suffer are doubly strong,
For ye know God strengtheneth those oppressed.
    Some day with mien affrighted,
And woful gesture, shall suppliant stand
Who so haughty is now, so proud and grand,
While the lifted finger of spectre hand
    Shall point to fair lives blighted.

Has he time to think of one growing old
Who counteth his money and hoards his gold?
Heaping the coffers, I fear me lest,
Perchance, his soul he has bartered and sold
For worldly lucre, so loved and caressed.
    Poor mortal, too short-sighted!

But the mills of the gods are grinding away ;
They move so slowly, impatient we say,
But the grist he brings shall be ground some day,
   Then shall he be requited.

God fitteth the back the burden to bear,
Though bending we droop under weight of care
Until, ah me, that it should be confessed,
Like merest dross is the glitter and glare
Gilding the surface of deepest unrest
   Termed life, when hopes are blighted,
And we bear a cross from day unto day.
That it may grow lighter we humbly pray,
As patient we tread our wearisome way,
   'Neath clouds of grief benighted.

In stillness of night comes a voice we know,
Whose tones thrilled our being long summers ago,
And these are the words of the angel guest :—
" Through meekness to grandeur the soul must grow.
Wouldst have thy spirit for evermore blest
   With heaven's glory lighted ?"
And the voice that speaks is the one we love,
Tenderer, sweeter, than coo of the dove ;
" He is just," it saith, " who reigneth above ;
   By Him shall wrong be righted."

IN VALE OF SORROW.

In vale of sorrow, and with mournful eyes,
   A poet stood submerged in depth of grief.
Emotion's fount was touched, and tears and sighs
   Rose from the heart, yet gave they no relief.

Depressed, disheartened, and with care bowed down,
   She felt the shadows thick about her fall;
She drooped like child beneath a parent's frown,
   And gloom enshrouded like a funeral pall.

And thus she wept; the tears like falling rain
   Came welling forth with surging throb and moan,
With mystic longing and a yearning pain,
   Intense intensity by poets known.

Then strove she, though with faltering strength and feet,
   To climb the hill, to reach the height aloft;
To find the purer air indeed were sweet.
   Vain the attempt; she backward fell, and oft.

But soon the fluttering of unseen wings,
   Descending from the glorious starry sphere,
Fanning like breath the summer zephyr brings,
   Brought balm of peace, and dried the poet's tear.

She felt the presence of an unseen guest;
   She heard the whisperings of angel voice.
The heart is solaced that was sore oppressed,
   And e'en the burdened soul must now rejoice.

So, spirit-strengthened, yet again she tried
   To climb the mount, to reach the sunny slope,
Upborne, surrounded as on either side
   By waving wings of Faith and Love and Hope.

For now, behold, as answer to her prayer
   The heavenly muse the poet stooped to bless,
And gave two strong, bright pinions pure and fair—
   Endowed the mourner thus with sweet caress.

Then rose the singer through the ether sea,
   Beyond the clouds that seemed so dark and dread,
And sent her song exultantly and free,
   Gladsome as sunlight beaming overhead.

And thus in purer air the soul beams forth;
  To clouded lives brings radiant holy light,
A benediction to sad hearts on earth,
  To guide them upward to the untrod height.

With flood of music poet-souls outpour
  In song and anthem other souls may rise
To realms of thought, in charmèd mystic lore,
  To revel in the poet's paradise.

Aye, gifted one, on pinions airy rise,
  Attaining altitude of heights sublime.
Where reigns fore'er the love that never dies,
  Space hath no bounds, nor cycle is to time.

MEMORY.

She sits in the shade of a darkened room,
Surrounded by warp and woof of the loom.
She weaves, with wonderful magical art,
Bright pictures of joy, sweet dreams of the heart;
The thoughts in mind that rise and tell
Of visions of beauty that with her dwell.
She's a beautiful being—truthful and pure.
Her fabric, as lasting as life, will endure.
I feel to-night all of witchery's spell
E'er cast over those who with memory dwell.

In a low, sweet voice she tenderly trills;
To the musical rhythm our being thrills.
All our senses they lave, the ebb and flow
Of waves of the beautiful "long ago."
The sacredest chamber in every heart
Is ever for memory set apart—

Returns to our mind, while weaving she sings;
The long-ago pleasures again she brings.
Should we shut her out from her place in the heart,
She knocks for entrance and will not depart.
Her angel presence of beauty and truth
Is solace to age and pleasure to youth.

She gives back the long-gone days that had fled,
And paths where our young feet hastened to tread;
The scenes that were brightest, the things most dear,
In beautiful patterns she weaves them here.
With her I oft linger, as in a dream,
O'er things that have been, but now only seem.
I yearningly gaze, as with memory I come,
On web-woven pictures wrought by her loom,
As she lifts the ideal fabric to view,
Portraying our past, so lifelike and true.

She has blended together light and shade;
In wonderful texture, her hands have made
Just here a bright pattern, sunbeams, and flowers,
A vision so fair of childhood's bright hours;
And a golden web she faithfully weaves
Of joyous youth, with a border of leaves;
And the sunniest days, of childhood's glee
And youth's bright hours, she pictures for me;
And I seem to stroll in reveries sweet
Through the path where o'erhanging branches meet.

All the past returns, the present recedes;
I gather the daisies that sprinkle the meads.
The flowers of hope in profusion lie there,
Intwined with the garland of love bright and fair.
Hope's buds here sometimes lie scattered and dead,
And weeds of despair grow rankly instead.
Many pictures thus hang on memory's wall,
And the gray mist of time ever veils them all.

5

Most beautiful ones that fairest unfold
Are woven of memory's threads of gold.
Their frames are of fanciful texture wove,
Of flowers of beauty, of hope, and love.

And as quickly as I before them pass,
She covers each scene with magical glass.
A mirror reflecting, it backward brings
Long-vanished years on their fast flying wings.
Like wingèd mile-posts, each swift passing year
Was marked with sorrow, a smile, or a tear.
Memory lifts her voice and sweetly will sing
Of dear forms and scenes she only can bring;
Then she turns to her loom, and, weaving anew,
Fair forms and loved faces she bringeth to view.

Here's a spray of flowers her fingers have wrought,
That grew in the beautiful garden of thought.
With threads of a dream the garland is twined;
Again by her wonderful sway o'er the mind,
The spell her magic hath over us cast;
We review with her the scenes of the past.
She sings "long ago" to a thought beating time,
And measures the weft by the poet's own rhyme;
Then touching our heart-strings, maketh them thrill
By magical grace of her own sweet will.
She reacheth our mind, and bids it awake,
From lethargic sleep our senses would take.
She leads us to gaze on work she hath wrought,
The long-vanished scenes her genius hath caught.

The leaves in the book of our life are portrayed
With the woof and the warp, and the light and shade—
Thoughts and feelings as well, and flights of time.
Inclosed in a mystic border of rhyme;
The pain and the anguish of by-gone years,
She weaves them all in with sorrow and tears,

A sombre tint for the deserts we've crossed,
Great waves of grief where our soul hath been tossed.
Here's a fairy barge with hope's banners decked,
And gulf of despair where the boat was wrecked.
Now a grassy green mound she pictures here—
For the loved and the lost are to memory dear.

Now her shuttle she fills with deeper dyes,
And weaves in the glance of bonny bright eyes,
Or a sunny curl, or a dimpled cheek,
Or a pensive smile, so winning and meek ;
And again she weaves, with a golden thread,
The brightest hopes that forever have fled.

As sweet, sad thoughts come with echo's refrain,
With rapturous thrill she endows us again.
How dear is her presence, who, dwelling apart,
Lingers to bless us in depth of our heart !
Her form hath a magical, nameless grace ;
She rules us, a queen, in her God-given place.

Truth twined the garland enwreathing her brow.
She reaches my mind ; she is swaying it now ;
She causeth the color to come and go
On the cheek, like the ceaseless ebb and flow
Of waves on the beach or the pebbly strand,
Embracing, receding, and kissing the land.
Who dwelleth with memory shall see and know
And recall the visions of long ago,
For fabrical scrolls by memory unfurled
Bring visions and joys of a hidden world.

Glance through her glass at her pictures, and see
Sweet thoughts and sad ones she bringeth to thee.
Yield thou to the spell which she casteth o'er me—
Aye, blessed forever shall memory be !

CHARITY.

She's a friend indeed, a friend in need ;
She hath no lengthened and tiresome screed,
But kindness in word and thought and deed
Is what she teacheth—the only creed
      Of Charity.

She giveth good words that ever are fraught
With priceless treasures of kindly thought ;
Thus laden with comfort that cannot be bought
Are the cheering words that ever are brought
      By Charity.

She healeth the wounded hearts that bleed ;
She heareth the yearning of hearts that plead ;
She answers with generous act and deed,
And hastens the hungering ones to feed,
      Doth Charity.

She helpeth the faltering step to sustain ;
She bringeth a solace for sorrow and pain ;
She forgiveth a wrong yet again and again ;
She harbors no malice ; that cannot remain
      With Charity.

Another's misfortune she'll ever deplore ;
She refuseth her mercy to none who implore ;
She turneth no wanderer from her door ;
She gives what she can, with a will to give more,
      Doth Charity.

She for wretched and outcast doth sympathy feel ;
By dying bedside doth praying kneel ;
The record of errors she will not reveal,
But close it with silence—the tender seal
      Of Charity.

Encouraging words most kindly to speak,
To shelter God's lambs from the winds so bleak,
To help the needy, protect the weak,
Aye, this is the mission, if mission you seek,
   Of Charity.

The naked are clothed, the hungry are fed,
And ministers sent to the dying bed,
And, when the life-light forever hath fled,
Then tenderly closed are the eyes of the dead
   By Charity.

Upholding the feeble lest they shall fall,
Never neglecting the sufferer's call,
She entereth hovels where woe doth appall
The bravest of hearts, for greatest of all
   Is Charity.

Her platform is broad, her precepts will win:
She teacheth that all in the world are akin;
Her religion will take all humanity in;
A mantle that covers a mountain of sin
   Hath Charity.

And, ever remember, the Scriptures say
That with you the poor ye must have alway.
Take heed to the call of the needy, I pray,
And minister to them from day to day
   With Charity.

Your giving shall be your goodliest gain;
"Cast on the waters," your bread will sustain
Some famishing life, and return again
From grateful hearts you have rescued from pain,
   By Charity.

Aye, blessed shall be unwearying feet,
That stay not their steps for the rain or sleet,

But haste the demands of hunger to meet;
They will find a rest and recompense sweet
   Through Charity.

And blessed are they who ever will find
In their thoughts a kindness for all mankind,
For this is the brotherly tie that doth bind,
The lovers of God, whose hearts are inclined
   To Charity.

Then bring to her temple no meagre dole,
And angels above shall your names enroll
In letters of gold on a mystic scroll;
She strengthens the body and saves the soul,
   Doth Charity.

Let generous thoughts and actions accord.
Who gives to the needy lends to the Lord;
Deep down in your heart this proverb record :·
Who lendeth to Him shall win a reward
   For Charity.

NATURE'S BOOK.

How strange is life, and how God's wondrous plan
Is wrought, distorted by the hands of man.
How many wheels, with many a wheel inside,
That mind of man may never truly guide.
How many blundering steps we take in life,
And how we need a helping hand through strife
Of weary days; and how, in lonely hour,
We long for kindred soul that hath the power
To cheer our pathway, as in gloom of night
A shipwrecked sailor longeth for the light.

How many sad mistakes in life are seen.
In contrast strange, what is—what might have been!
What motor, then, shall sway the mind of man,
And work out life by great Jehovah's plan,
Till, well adjusted, every wheel in use
Shall move all smoothly, shielded from abuse?
Alas, strange contradiction! man's a fool,
Who, ruled by nature, still would nature rule ;
And so perchance he gives a careless look,
A passing glance will take at nature's book,
Thinking, perhaps, he's read the page aright.
Warped images he sees, through blinded sight.
But when he breaks her universal laws,
Experience shows, in nature's book, the cause
For deepest sorrow.   If with eyes grown dim
Her page he truly reads, 'twere well for him.
God's plan is perfect.   Nature holds the key,
Though worldly wise refuse its loveliness to see.
With cunning art society would rule
And sway the mass—a hollow creed her school.
Who enters there must henceforth play the fool ;
Conventional his style henceforth must be.
He's fashion slave, ruled by society.
What wonder then the leaves of life unfurled
To nature false, show touch of crafty world!
So wandering feet forever go astray
When nature's voice, and lesson she would say,
Is heeded not—earth's children disobey.
Who wrongs himself can never make amends,
Yet thrice thyself than once do wrong to friends.
If passion guides and leads the way to sin,
Who makes the bed must lie content therein ;
And just as well might hawk be termed a dove
As base-born passion bear the name of love.
Who hears through nature God's mysterious voice
His heart will thrill and evermore rejoice—
The chords of sympathy vibrate with lasting joy.
A kindred heart brings bliss without alloy.

Then let us strive to learn God's perfect plan—
Work out our mission, filling out life's span,
And make our creed the Brotherhood of Man.
Heaven grant that we whose paths have not been bright
May still look up and read God's works aright.

"WOMAN'S SPHERE." *

I STUDIED human rights and pondered long
Ere first I lifted up my voice in song,
Whose burden was the weight of woman's wrong;
For sympathy doth help oppressed be strong.

The grieved refrain went forth most sad and low,
And met an answering echo from the long ago,
When others thought and sang whose race was run,
Whose task was ended, ere mine had begun.

Rolled backward and unfurled the scroll of time,
In measured movement, like the poet's rhyme;
Whereon was limned, I saw through unshed tears,
Some panoramic views of twoscore years.

I saw a group, a handful they, so few,
Of earnest women, brave, with purpose true;
Who claimed, for which the scoffer them abused,
That God gave talent that it might be used.

And then I heard, borne westward, from the sea,
These words, wind-wafted, "justice, equity,"
And this the motto on their faces writ,
The which I conned—in mind I treasured it.

---

* Read before the National Woman Suffrage Convention in Washington City, January 19, 1881.

These patient, earnest women in their lives
Performed their parts, as maidens, mothers, wives,
Yet found they time to combat public wrong,
To vindicate the right became more strong.

And sad indeed, a sight so strange to see,
To ask for justice brings them contumely;
Laughed at as weak, injustice seeks to find
A sword, in ridicule, cries "strong of mind."

That those who learn at faithful mother's knee
How strong and true her thoughtful love can be—
Most sad that these should in derision speak
Of mental strength; pray would they have mind weak?

They counselled then, for strength, and went their way;
Then passed the scene, and came another day.
I see a structure, looming grand and fair,
A fount of knowledge, and men enter there.

Here skill attain; Science doth here mature
Her pupils, that by healing art may cure.
Now came these women; "we will learn," said they,
"To lighten pain, the hand of death to stay."

And then they knocked for entrance, knocked in vain;
The doors are closed, and thus do they remain.
A voice is heard as coming from within,
"Where Esculapius reigns ye go not in.

"Ye are but women! women come not here!
For science lies not in a woman's sphere."

Their brothers entered and came forth again
Enlightened—to be famous; they were men.
Oh bigotry! that would the mind encrust
With inactivity and slothful rust.

These sisters knocked again; they sure must win;
The door's ajar!   Lo, one has entered in.
By perseverance others, now in this domain,
A thousand licensed are to lighten pain.

My heart was gladdened when I saw this band
Gaining in numbers, keeping hand in hand,
Approach the dome where justice doth preside,
And ask for entrance there.   It was denied.

They pleaded, " Let us help the laws to frame
That govern *us*. Justice, 'tis all we claim."
Response came not, and thus they asked again :
" Let us then study, practice law like men."

And then a voice so low I scarce could hear,
As 'twere ashamed of words that now appear,
Said, " Ye have mercy, more than justice knew ;
And ye have pity, too, accorded you."

Was brought to mind then one who thought the laws
Should women learn, *provided*—add this clause—
She practice not—he gravely said, because
She might write speeches *for him*, keep her sphere,
Save him, he guessed, two hundred pounds a year.

Yet voices strong, from realms of legal lore ;
(Not world outside) came sternly as before :
" Not here, not here, ye cannot enter here ;
We make good laws *for* you—have not a fear—
But *legal ken* is not in ' woman's sphere.' "

Came transformation.   Women then I saw,
Amenable to man-made, civil law,
Unjust, oppressive, taxed for government,
Bound by a code they did not represent.

Saw them as culprits, mercy whispering low,
" Poor women ;" echoed pity, " Let them go !"
And thus I knew in courts were women tried,
With mercy given, yet justice oft denied.

And now behold, I see a valorous few
Have passed the door of legal knowledge through.
Some followed soon ; now scattered, there and here
Are women lawyers, of their brothers peer,
And yet they cry, *This is not woman's sphere.*

I saw tall spires and lofty structures rise,
As lifting incense to the upper skies ;
With windows stained, and richly wrought within
The altars these, to save a world from sin.

Here truths were taught, of Him who reigns above—
Of Christ the merciful, a *God of love.*
Here women wished to lift their voice, and teach ;
Men said, " *Keep silence; women must not preach.*"

Then I rebelled against the narrow creed,
Though Bishop Simpson did most bravely plead
For woman's entrance; thirty years he sought
To make her *teacher* where she hath been taught.

And some, whose hearts a holy zeal hath fired,
Did lift the voices that were Heaven inspired.
Great-souled philanthropist, Lucretia Mott,
Her inspiration lives, though *she is not.*

And yet, when women thought to preach and pray,
The bell pealed forth, and pealing seemed to say :
" Not here ; not here ; ye cannot enter here,
Not here ; the pulpit is not woman's sphere."

I saw the throng press forward, at the door
Of various buildings knock as erst before ;

And some made plea—refused as soon as made—
To gain admittance there, and learn a trade.

Was heard then many voices from within:
"Brothers are we," sounded o'er noisy din
And hum of wheels. "No room for women here.
Not here, not here; this is not woman's sphere."

Yet some gained entrance, and employment they
Were given, by asking, taking lesser pay,
And various crafts were taught, and learned to wield
The shuttle, pen, and type in labor's field,
Although the type clicked out "Not here; not here!"
A treadle creaked and squeaked "Not here, thy sphere!"

I queried then who made—what is her sphere?
A manly voice replied, his answer here:
"Her sphere, her sphere, why, that is very plain.
Her sphere is home, and there should she remain.

"Ye must admit that 'tis her destiny,
Since she alone can wife or mother be.
A husband, father, I, 'tis also true,
Yet various rounds of action I pursue.

"A woman's sphere, 'tis very clear to see,
Since I a wife or mother cannot be,
These duties hers, whate'er I cannot do,
For should I else, perhaps, assume them too."
The chorus join "not here, not here, not here,"
And leave to woman scarce a hemi—sphere.

And now where erst for right a score had stood—
For years had passed—battling for womanhood,
Thousands of faces rise, with silvery hair,
Grown gray in service—others young and fair.

The work they wrought on scroll of time appeared,
The schools, the college, homes, their hands have reared.
A million enter strong in hand and heart
The fields of labor, learning, science, art.

Dear Stanton, loved, for whom old time hath spun
A snowy crown, it was most dearly won,
Yet brave and strong, defender true, have we.
Heaven bless the noble helper, Susan Anthony.

Men *mean* us well, but give so little heed
To what is just, or of what we have need;
They cannot know that many a woman's mind
Preys on itself, so closely 'tis confined.

And thousands, women waiting to be free,
Lift patient glances, yet men will not see
Are fettered women pleading o'er the land.
Men are not fettered—cannot understand.

They need our aid in Government 'tis true;
Yet say, "ask freedom," mock us when we do.
They scarce believe high Heaven ordained that we
Be equal.   Justice yields equality.

We work out our salvation, bravely do
The things we can, and best are fitted to,
And we, in time not very far remote—
In this free land—we women mean to *vote*.

The scroll is folded, once again I hear
A voice inspired, the prophecy of seer.
A million voices echo—" *Time is near*
When woman draws that magic line, her sphere."

ONLY A DREAM.

ONLY a dream,
Beautiful dream,
Like the last faint ray of the sunset's gleam—
Airiest fancy, beautiful theme—
Shadows they are, yet so real they seem,
Brightest of visions, how real ye seem!

Over the sky
Fleecy clouds fly;
So in our dreaming the fancies float by;
Flitting like breath of a midsummer sigh,
As love-light that beams in the glance of an eye.
Why must they vanish, oh, why! tell me why?

Empyrean dye—
Azure so high—
The glories of heaven, thy tints underlie.
It seemeth sometimes thou art coming more nigh.
Only a dream! Thou art ever as high.
My longing may reach thee, perhaps, by and by.

Dream, faintest glint
Of sunshine, a hint
That grief on the soul will leave its imprint,
As the impress is stamped by the die of the mint,
A lingering echo, a sad, sober tint,
The impress of a shadowy hint.

The fairy-like trace
Of delicate lace,
Or beautiful landscape on window-glass;
The net-work King Frost weaves of mimicry's grace
Will vanish as beauty fades out from a face.
So sunbeams dispel dreams as shadows they chase.

Dreaming for years,
    Dreaming, though tears
Steal forth from closed eyelids ; yet sorrow endears,
As still in the mind a loved scene reappears ;
Long agone dreams the heart ever reveres.
Though they vanish, they teach us to banish our fears.

Still may I dream,
    Still may I deem
Thou art mine own, as in dreaming doth seem.
Though hope even fade as the sunset's last gleam,
Still in my mind airy fancies will teem,
And memory cherish the beautiful dream.

A SONG OF THE SOUL.

DEDICATED TO J. G. WHITTIER.

A SINKING sun with beams aslant
    Tingeing with gold the clouds on high ;
Like dream of loveliness, doth haunt,
    Yet saddens me, I scarce know why.

The purpling splendor of the scene,
    The light that floods the sunset skies
Uplift my soul, and yet, I ween
    Not why, these wayward tears will rise.

Perchance from some divine despair
    Whose depth no plummet-line may sound,
Welling beneath a surface fair,
    The source of these, my tears, is found.

For true it is, as summer eve
    In golden glory glides to rest,
Then grieve I as a child might grieve
    When taken from its mother's breast.

'Tis nature's joy of grief, I trow,
   Thrilling with pleasant pain, my heart,
Stirring the fountain's limpid flow,
   Forcing reluctant tears to start.

Would I might weave some sweet refrain,
   Like sunset 'neath a cloud of gray,
Or thrill the heart with Orphic strain,
   Enchanting as the closing day.

God's smiling face appears to me
   Beyond the glow of setting sun,
And very near, I seem to see
   The heavenly goal, now almost won.

My heart may not the throb control
   That beats within this weary breast:
Nor may I calm this struggling soul
   That ever yearns to be at rest.

My longing thoughts in transports rise,
   Expanding in the purer air:
I view the rainbow-tinted skies,
   And would my life might be as fair.

With trembling shadows all my soul
   Is thickly cast and chequered o'er:
Yet still on high God's orb doth roll,
   That drives the shadows on before.

And when my life shall close its day—
   When all my earthly task is done—
May earth's fair scenes then fade away
   Serenely as the setting sun.

And when mine eyes grow dim in death,
   Then may my spirit, pure, and fair,
Soar upward with my latest breath,
   Rise heavenward on the evening air.

Borne upward through the ether sea,
  Beyond the circumambient skies,
Released, my soul, exultant, free,
  Shall with the sun of glory rise.

SOME DAY.

WHISPER in accents low,
    Some day,
    Gladly,
Thou lovest me more than aught below;
    Some day,
When ruddy cheek hath lost its glow,
    And I am old,
Thy strong arms then around me fold,
Loving me then as now.
Oh, darling! love me so.

When I am lying low,
    Some day,
    Sadly,
Then, thou shalt surely know,
    Some day,
My life doth outward flow,
    Like ebbing tide.
Sit, then, my dying couch beside,
Smoothing my fevered brow;
I shall more quiet grow.

When painful angry throe,
    Some day,
    Madly,
Chaseth my life-blood till it cease to flow;
    Some day,
When aching heart shall throb so slow,

6

My wasted cheek
Kiss then, and lips that cannot speak,
Blessing by silent vow,
Love, bless me ere I go.

When fragrant zephyrs blow,
  Some day,
  Sadly,
Sighing a requiem soft and low ;
  Some day,
Swaying the leaves so mournfully and slow ;
  There I shall seem
To rise before you, as in a dream,
Over the spot where weeping willows bow,
And where sweet wild-flowers grow.

When fading sunset's glow,
  Some day,
  Redly,
Casteth a parting gleam ere sinking low ;
  Some day,
Above my grave, bending in voiceless woe,
  Or kneeling there,
Breathing a loving, silent prayer,
To that low mound come thou,
Sobbing, " I loved her so !"

Though when, I may not know ;
  Some day,
  Sadly,
When I lie sleeping the green turf below—
  Some day
Thy anguished tears shall flow ;
  When I have passed away,
Shall memory touch thy heart, some day,
Then thou wilt say—oh ! why not now ?—
" Dear one, I love thee *so !*"

GRANT.

BEAR the great warrior to the silent tomb:
Life's siege is ended. Lay him gently down
To rest eternal. The lips, whose lightest word
Was as a signal of command, a mandate given,
Fore'er are stilled.

The eagle eyes, whose fearless glance hath thrilled
And urged to patriot deed the multitude,
Are closed in dreamless sleep.

The giant mind, that marshalled mighty forces
And sent forth troops of vigilant thoughts
With action armed, forestalling action,
Hath ceased to act.

The modern Hercules, whose massive strength
Hath moved the Western World of valiant men ;
Whose word hath swayed its legionry of peoples ;
Whose sword hewed paths to loftiest achievements ;
The soldier grand—he of the cloudless brow—
Lies prone and powerless.

A ruler wise and just, obeyed and loved ;
Honored by all the nations of the earth ;
For whom "death had no sting," the grave no conquest,
Hath laid the sceptre down.

Revered by countless armies he hath led ;
Mourned by a million brother comrades ;
Wearing the laurels of immortal fame ;
Draped in the starry folds his courage saved ;
In hearts innumerable the "Old Commander"
In deathless glory lives.

His mantle, fold about him—none can wear it,
His sword, lay by his side—there's none to wield it.
Who fought for Union's life triumphantly,
Now shorn of strength, lies at his Maker's feet.
A world bowed o'er a grave, is wrapped in grief:
A Hero's dead! A Chieftain's fallen!

INSANITY.

A SKETCH.

I'm mad! mad! mad! I know but this—I'm mad!
My 'wildered brain doth ever seeth and boil
Like unto devil's broth in steaming caldron.
My mind is turmoil, and my thoughts are stirred
Into an endless maze of wild confusion,
And, as my fevered thoughts like vapors rise,
Or empty bubbles in uncertain flight.
I seek to reach, to guide and master them;
Yet, ere I have the power, they vanish
Quick as a meteor's flash, and all is dark.
Another riseth from my throbbing brain;
Brightness gleams upon its wavering surface
As though the mind itself were shining through.
How eagerly! aye, with what frantic haste
I try to grasp it; but, alas, it bursts,
Resolves itself to airy nothingness.
Again I blindly grope in utter darkness.
These scintillating bubbles from my mind
Thus rise and vanish in their aimless way.
Their course through space is never pointed out:
No plans, no future destiny have they,
And thus to me they vividly portray
My madness. And I know, I feel, I'm mad—

For what is madness?   'Tis the power lost
To train these flitting fancies of the brain;
To follow up our thoughts and still command—
Retain them as obedient servants.

But my mind hath had too many servants;
They have too well filled their allotted sphere;
They throng the temple, and they crowd the brain;
They beat upon the wall of mind; the wall
Gives way.   My mind is like a broken drum.
On which no more the echoing tones resound;
They surge, in maddening glee, or harsh uproar,
As ceaseless breakers dash on the rock-bound shore.

Yet they are strong; thoughts have become too strong;
They have o'erpowered me, and they are my masters.
I cannot, howe'er much I would, escape them:
Henceforth, like abject slave, or culprit whipped,
I do, I must, their woful, wicked bidding,
Although my weary step and haggard brow
Prove how my strength is taxed beyond endurance.
Yet still these wicked thoughts, like phantom forms,
Do drive me, whisper in my crazed ear,
Do this, do that, they say, or yet the other,
And taunt and sneer and make me fiend inhuman;
And though 'twere murder foul, or suicide,
I even must obey this mighty power,
This ghoul that hath me ever in its clutches,
As grip of Hercules, or iron vise,
From which no hand can save, no help avail.
No wrench, save that given by the hand of death,
　　　Can set my spirit free.

A CHILD WITH GOLDEN CURLS.

Thou hadst a shining pearl,
A fairy child, with floating golden curl,
 A gem that erst was thine.
Now, lifted up to heaven's light,
Thy pearl hath grown more pure, more bright,
 And shines with light divine.

Thou hadst a beauteous gem—
A rosebud, clinging to its parent stem
 From dewy morn till even;
Yet from its stem the bud was torn;
Thy heart, alas! is left to mourn—
 Thy rosebud blooms in heaven.

Thou hadst a little bird
Whose thrilling notes were sweetest ever heard;
 It nestled on thy breast:
Away from earthly care and sin.—
Heaven's portal ope'd—thy bird flew in;
 Thy heart's an empty nest.

Thou hadst, oh heart oppressed,
A lamb; 'tis folded on the Shepherd's breast:
 Away from care and strife,
Where pain and sorrow cannot come,
Thy lamb hath found a safer home,
 A purer, better life.

Thou hadst a prattling child,
Than which none fairer, sweeter, ever smiled:
 Too pure, too fair, for earth.
It lingered but a while to bless
Thy heart, whose yearning tenderness
 Through suffering finds new birth.

Thy soul must e'en look up,
Though to the dregs thou'st drained the bitter cup:
    Look up through clouds of grief;
Faith looks through tears to light above,
For God is e'er a God of love,
    And He will bring relief.

FLIGHT OF THE MUSE.

TO A POET OF THE EMERALD ISLE.

FAR away o'er the misty mountain,
    Where the tall pine moans and sways;
Far away where the woodland fountain
    In shade of the willow plays,

My thought, like sweet breath of the morning
    On pinions of fancy afar,
Is borne to the halo adorning
    The beam of a mythical star;

To realms which though only in seeming
    Exist in a charming ideal;
Unseen but in mystical dreaming,
    Too fair and too bright to be real;

Where heavenly visions are thronging
    To thrill with intense ecstasy;
To fill all my being with longing
    Their beauties more clearly to see.

But shadowy cloudlets are drifting
    Athwart the vision of life;
And darkness seems nevermore lifting
    The pall from wearisome strife.

In fancy I float to the mountain
　Parnassus, float over, far above ;
O'er cloudland and murmuring fountain,
　To the realm of the Master of Love.

I soar on swift, fearless pinion,
　Through the upper and purer air ;
Far away from the earth's dominion—
　Far away from the world of care.

The zephyr breathes ever the sighing
　Of the longing that fills my soul ;
The bird that most swiftly is flying,
　Less eagerly seeketh its goal.

Yet somewhere in ages hereafter,
　My thought like the wind, shall sway,
The gladsomest flow of my laughter,
　In fountains shall ripple and play.

My spirit shall poise o'er the mountains
　Serene as the moonbeam's clear ray,
And bathe in delectable fountains,
　When life's shadows have drifted away.

A SORTIE OF KING FIRE.

'Tis a Sabbath evening fair,
Peaceful quiet all the air
　Does pervade, does prepare
Every heart, and the chime
Of the church-bell says 'tis time
　For the hour of prayer.

Church-bells now have ceased to ring;
Hushed and still is everything;
  Holy quiet, peace doth bring,
To the heart and soul most near—
Peace, to one and all most dear,
  Round the heart doth cling.

Suddenly there sounds a cry
As of peril coming nigh;
  Whence the sound and what the cry,
What the danger, what the harm,
Menaced in that wild alarm?
  Tell us, passer-by.

Hark, the cry is "fire! fire!"
  Speeding fast by magic wire
The alarm flies to the tower;
Then the clanging bells join in,
Sound of hurrying, wrangling din
Rises higher still and higher,
  Like the raging fire.

Engines now and men so brave
Put forth all their power to save,
  And each burning building lave—
Drench and flood with water.
Fiery heat still waxes hotter;
Still the men work harder, faster;
But the fire still is master;
  Man is but its slave.

What is water, earth, or air?
How shall each or all compare,
  Or in battle shall they dare,
Rank above or equal fire?
Emulous but vain desire,
  They may not compare.

See it reaching, dancing, creeping,
Through the doors and windows leaping;
  Fire exults, though men be weeping
O'er the loss of wealth and power,
Swept from grasp within the hour,
  Swept by fire as now 'tis sweeping.

Iron fronts are forward bending,
Toppling walls are downward tending;
  Thrill of awe their fall is sending
To each heart—and over all
Cloud of flame and smoke doth fall,
  Added grandeur lending.

Still the men; in vain endeavor—
Like a power without a lever,
  With more courage men did never
Strive to conquer Fire.
Vain attempts and vain desire;
Now the wind is rising higher,
Reinforcement to the fire,
  Conquering now or never.

Heat intense and smoke as black
As Egypt's midnight, drive men back;
  Must they fail? Alas, alack—
Brave and true and faithful still;
Nerves of steel, and iron will,
Do their hopes at last fulfil—
  Cause the fire to slack.

Now the wind is sobbing, sighing,
For the fire at last is dying,
  Mid its smouldering ruins lying;
Fiercest flames are backward driven;
Fire's death-blow has been given,
  Therefore, wind, thy sighing.

Grandest glory has King Fire,
Mingling in his funeral pyre,
   Arches, roofs, and lordly hall,
   Iron front and massive wall;
   Hanging black smoke over all,
   Like a mighty funeral pall,
O'er destruction dire,—
Handwork of King Fire.

LET KISSES CLOSE MINE EYES.

PLACE no dull clods, no metal weights upon mine open eyes,
   Through which the longing, yearning soul hath found a sure
      release,
And soareth upward through the blue, beyond empyrean skies,
   Fair as a feathery cloudlet, floating through realms of peace.

Press softly, gently down, mine eyes with tender seal of love ;
   Let no tears fall nor deeply grieve when I lie cold and dead,
But, oh, rejoice exultingly, bending my bier above,
   That hath been given surcease from pain to weary heart and
      head.

Rejoice henceforth forever that the throbbing hath been stilled,
   The wild tumultuous throbbing of the restless human heart,
Which neither rude adversity nor cruel world had chilled—
   In unison with Nature, seemed of Nature's self a part.

Rejoice that full emotion from its fount hath ceased to flow,
   Nor let thine own emotion sadly rise to make you weep ;
But press thy lips in thankfulness o'er eyelids drooping low,
   Thus let thy kisses fold them down—I shall more sweetly sleep.

CLOUD-LAND.

THE clouds, the beautiful clouds!
    Oh, could I but write,
    As I see them to-night!
The beautiful, varying clouds.

The clouds, ever-changing clouds,
    Floating airily by,
    Weaving webs in the sky—
The beautiful, silvery clouds.

The clouds, the mountainous clouds,
    Are uplifted so high
    In the blue of the sky—
The towering mountains of clouds.

The clouds, the luminous clouds,
    And clouds, like lace,
    Nearly veiling the face
Of the luminous, sunset clouds.

The clouds, most glorious clouds,
    Rising higher and higher—
    Great pillars of fire—
The grandest of glorious clouds.

The clouds, the terrible clouds!
    They gather and roll,
    Like despair o'er the soul—
Most terrible, threatening clouds!

The clouds, the storm-laden clouds,
    They with tear-drops of rain
    Moisten earth's face again,
The clouds, heavy rain-laden clouds.

The clouds, summer, sunset clouds,
 They are, after the rain,
 Golden burnished again,
By the sun peeping under the clouds.

The beautiful, beautiful clouds!
 Oh, could I but write,
 As I sit here to-night,
All the grandeur, the beauty of clouds!

THE JUDGE.

Ah! that the Judge, so great in mind,
In judgment were a trifle kind;
And being Judge, full well he must
Fulfil his part—be not unjust,
Nor malice prepense hold should he;
(The Judge and I might then agree.)
I much admire his sparkling wit,
Or manly, upright "shoulder hit."
Ah! would that wit included praise,
Which but a censuring thought displays.
Oft hidden satire lurks within
Bland words, that form a covering thin:
Expressions soft from smiling lip,
Like gloved hand, hide a painful grip.
And surely no one should object
To greet the power of intellect;
We like the brilliant *jeu d'esprit*,
And mark the ready repartee.
E'en irony might not be bad,
(If one were only iron-clad,)
But caustic wit none can admire,
While every "burned child dreads the fire."

Far rather give a " cut direct"
Than cutting words for mere effect.
It does require a deal of nerve
To bear the blame we least deserve.
The tender plant asks gentle touch
Or suffers.   Does it ask too much?
In all his " charges" right and just
A judge should be, will be, I trust.
There is a mantle pure and fair
Which each and all of us should wear.

Judge this, not by the general rule,
That every poet is a fool ;
If poets lack sometimes in sense,
Their sense-itiveness is immense.
They suffer from the chilling blast
Of sarcasm, ever sweeping past.
The tender plant asks gentle touch
Or suffers—'tis not asking much.
From lamb that's shorn the wind we shield ;
The heart is bare, its thoughts revealed ;
A store of thought and feelings true,
Pure pearls, the poet brings to you.
Be mindful of the tender thought,
Or all its wealth avails you naught.
The gold that's hidden under ground,
Is for a purpose, coined, when found ;
So hidden wealth of heart and mind
Is coined in words to help mankind.
A tender thought, expression given,
Does sometimes bring us nearer heaven.
A writer may his duty do
If to himself and others true,
And he who feels his motive pure
Much good may do, much ill endure.
If ye have talent, then, deserve ;
By use its shine undimmed preserve.

Of others' feelings have a care,
Yet in the right just do, and dare.
Than these no truer thoughts e'er wed:
"Be sure you're right," and "go ahead;"
And surely none there are but know
That friction makes pure metal glow.
Talent, though sometimes much abused,
Bright lustre sheds when rightly used;
Let not rust its bright surface dim,
But let its light reflect on Him.
Prosperity I envy none,
No more than star might envy sun.
All may not in the sunshine bask—
Some of us work at life-long task;
So oft denied, we long to hear
Kind words of praise or words of cheer,
Which make our life-work somewhat light,
And e'en the future seem more bright.
But justice should not be denied;
The Court should not the law o'erride.
The golden rule did all apply
How few would then for justice cry.
The "Judge is just," then let him feel
The truth set forth in this appeal,
And let him not, whate'er he do,
Another's motive misconstrue.
Nor praise nor censure I bespeak,
"Justice to all" is all I seek.

ALONE.

As suffering I lie on my couch to-day
   I long for the clasp of a vanished hand—
A step that has passed from the portal away—
   The love that encompassed our household band.

That harbored from harm in the dear home fold,
  With care so strong yet tender to see—
The family group, for we were, all told,
  The two little ones and myself, but three.

But death took from us our sheltering stay—
  The warm glowing heart that loved us so much;
I grieve in silence each wearisome day
  For comfort that lay in that vanished touch.

The grasp of a hand, now folded for aye—
  The face hidden deep from my gaze, for years;
Lo, wearisome weights on my eyelids lie,
  Whose lashes grow heavy with unshed tears.

'Tis hard that a woman must brave the world—
  So hard to do battle for daily bread.
If death's fatal dart at me had been hurled
  It were well I had died in his stead.

With patience, through trials I learn to be strong,
  And meet the rude conflict as best I can;
'Midst the jostling of worldly-minded throng,
  I wish for strength and assertion of man.

The wee ones he left me grow large and fair;
  A mother's great duty I feel and see;
I long, but in vain, for the tender care,
  The love that so guarded and sheltered me.

THE ISLAND HOME.

Dear Nature doth smile on a peaceful Isle
  Where dwelleth a poet and sage.
His anchorite life is devoid of strife;
  Love's grand lessons his thoughts engage.

Here the waters divide as onward they glide
  To encircle the charmèd spot;
With a dance and song they hasten along
  And meet at the foot of the grot.
On the island's shore, united once more
  They join in mellifluous race;
With wave after wave, the river doth lave—
  Caressing with laughing embrace.
Near the island's edge are thickets of sedge
  Where groweth the tree and the vine,
Where gray rabbits hide and nestlings abide;
  The tendril doth lovingly twine.
Here the vagrant breeze lifts twigs of the trees
  And the zephyr whispereth low,
While musical notes from soft feathered throats
  Oft blend with the murmuring flow.
All the dewy air is tremulous there
  With carol of many a bird,
And insects astir with humming and whir
  In myriad of sounds are heard.
And the crickets beat, and the lambkins bleat
  Like the pendulous throb in air.
The dove's tender coo and the night bird's, too,
  Proclaim a most wonderful care.
Away from the strife of turbulent life,
  And caressed by Heaven's pure breeze,
Near the sunny gleam of the flowing stream,
  And sheltered by forest-trees—
Like a maiden I ween, white-robed and serene—
  A home on the island doth rise,
Where in peaceful content life's evening is spent
  By the sage who is lovingly wise.
Marbled forms here are from countries afar,
  From regions of classical lore,
And art treasures fair, unique, and most rare,
  Comprising a wonderful store.
Here in shelfy nooks repose precious books,
  Till thousands are marshalled in line.

7

They are rich, I ween, with legend and scene
  And a wit that sparkles like wine.
A brilliant mind, fair, and a genius rare
  That home like a safe casket holds;
A brow that the gems of the diadems
  In the poet's crown, enfolds.
Oh, silvery wave, oh, waters that lave,
  Let joy sound your roundelay, still!
Oh, birdlings so fair, let pulsate the air
  To charm him with merriest trill.
Oh, fairest flowers, enwreath the bowers,
  Attired in your loveliest dress,
And Heaven's fair breeze and soft zephyrs, please.
  Waft o'er him your lightest caress.
Oh, Father above, preserve him in love
  And pillow his head on your breast;
From the Island Home, when the time has come,
  Transfer him to Heavenly rest.

A FAREWELL TO SIGHT.*

DEAR Lord, and must it, can it be
That I no more again shall see?
    No more forever—
The earth's soft carpet, brightly green,
Or watch the wavering, shimmering sheen
    Play o'er the river?

* "A lady near Covington, Kentucky, whose sight was failing, upon consulting a physician was told that in a few hours she would be totally blind. She went home, took a farewell look at familiar objects, and had her two little children dressed in their prettiest attire and brought before her, that, as the light faded from her eyes, their latest sight should rest on them."

No more the fragrant spring-time flowers
That erstwhile gave me many hours
　　Of sweet delight—
Nor mossy banks 'neath shady trees
With leaflets swaying in the breeze
　　Shall glad my sight.

No more my upward gaze shall rest
Upon the towering mountain's crest
　　Grand and sublime—
Nor watch the singing, rippling rill
Flow swiftly 'neath the rocky hill
　　Ceaseless as time.

I'll see no more the waving grain,
Nor vessels riding o'er the main
　　Of broad expanse.
No more these longing eyes shall look
On scenes of life from nature's book—
　　Not e'en a glance.

No more the cattle o'er the dale,
Nor cot half hidden in the vale,
　　The scene (for me) enhance
No sight of glorious works of art,
Nor nature's pictures fill my heart,
　　My soul entrance.

No more I'll see the sun uprise,
Nor e'er again, with beaming eyes,
　　Meet his bright beams—
For as he slowly sinks from sight
My sight goes also; I, ere night,
　　See but in dreams.

Bring now my precious treasures here,
My darling babes, so fair, so dear,
　　Their childish grace—

That I may linger fondly o'er
Each lineament; in my mind may store
    Each pictured face.

Robed in pure vestment fair and white,
Thus let them fade from loving sight,
    Like sun at even—
My heart shall watch them day by day,
Though eyes see not—them, I will pray
    To see in heaven.

THE CHILD AND THE CONVICT.

Oh, prisoner with the weary air,
    That seems an unbreathed sigh,
And brow marked o'er with furrowing care,
    And deep despondent eye,

What means the sudden look that gleams,
    Brightens thine eye with light,
That paints thy face with feeling—seems
    Like day-dawn after night?

What dost thou see?   A little child,
    Led by a mother's hand;
An infant girl in features mild
    Moves through this prison band.

This is the chord that touched thy heart
    And gave thine eye-beams birth;
This is the light of love, the part
    That glorifies the earth.

And, oh, that eager, yearning look!
  It thrills us like a tone;
We read it like a printed book,
  And it becomes our own.

We note the look of mute appeal,
  Interpret as we ought;
We know, we think, we read, we feel,
  We reach thy inmost thought.

Our hearts with kindred feelings swell;
  We read with nature's art:
Thou hadst a child, thou know'st the spell
  That 'thralls the father's heart.

Convict and stranger though thou art,
  And outcast though thou be,
A little child can reach thy heart,
  Show there pure thoughts to me.

WE IDLED A SEASON AWAY.

WHEN many a year has vanished,
  And life nears the close of its day,
We will treasure the sweet communings
  That hastened a summer away.

We talked and thought of the future,
  Yet hoped not for worldly bliss;
But heavenly homes we would win us,
  By filling our mission in this.

If I in my rhyming idyls
  Have taught you the good and the true,
The season you thought was barren
  Brought harvests of knowledge to you.

We know that rich pearls of wisdom
  May fall from the lips of a child.
A womanly child may God keep me,
  From snares of this world undefiled.

Long after the summer hath faded,
  And the winter of death has come;
May we meet in the golden city,
  And spend one long summer at *home.*

PEARLS OF THOUGHT.

With head low bowed, and eyelids heavy laden—
  With grief and sorrow and fast-falling tears,
Tired and footsore, seeking distant Aidenn,
  I wander through the path of weary years.
The way is rough, the clouds are black around me,
  Temptation's dragon still besets my path.
Trials and dangers, like the clouds, surround me,
  And smother, like the deadly simoon's breath.
An arid desert I have crossed, affliction.
  Experience has led me by the hand.
His lamp he loaned me; by its faint reflection
  I found some thought-pearls on the desert sand;
And some were clear and delicate in tinting,
  And over some a darker shade was cast,
As seared fire, whose scorch had left imprinting,
  Or fiery breath had dimmed them as it passed.
But over all I found some hope-rays shining,
  Which gave new beauty to each added gem,
And roused me from my grief and sad repining,
  To weave the thought-pearls in a diadem.
The gems I gathered patiently I sought;
  Well-laden, from the blinding sands I rose,
And, lifting up to heaven my pearls of thought,
  Behold, each one thereafter fairer grows.

Not mine the thoughtless, joyous, happy ringing
   Of careless glee, or gayety and mirth.
In low, sad tones my brooding heart is singing;
   Like wounded bird, I hover near the earth.
Had I not walked through suffering and sadness,
   The pearly gems that beam with light divine
I ne'er had gathered—gems of chastened gladness,
   Nor would the priceless treasure, thought, been mine.
I sowed the tears—they were the overflowing
   Of deep emotion from my stricken heart—
But I could ne'er believe till now the sowing
   Would richest harvest, purest joy, impart.
Whence come these pearly gems? What magic brought them
   To mingle with affliction's desert waste?
In rich domains have many vainly sought them—
   The pearls of thought which in the diadem are placed,
They grow not in the garden of fruition;
   For hope fulfilled ne'er gave a thought-pearl birth.
Though wealth may seek, or fame, or high position,
   Their price is tears, a head low-bowed to earth.
The wounded bivalve in the depth of ocean
   May from that wound a pearly gem bring forth:
So hearts when pierced and trembling with emotion
   To peerless, priceless gems of thought give birth.
One way we have, one only way of knowing
   How bitter drops when spilled from too full cup,
Through nights of grief the tears to gems are growing;
   They are the seed from which pure pearls spring up.
If I at length shall reach a green oasis
   In desert life, whose fount may cheer and bless
My thirsting heart, I'll lift a song of praises,
   And thread my pearls, erst tears of bitterness.

TO A PICTURE.

I LOOK upon this pictured face,
  Shaded with quiet tender thought,
And wonder how a spirit's grace
  May be by artist's magic caught.

I look again, and dimly see
  A thought, expression, like my own;
And yet, I think it scarce can be
  Myself upon the canvas shown.

For this is far more fair than I,
  And bears imprint of ancient times,
Like dream of fair Italia's sky,
  Or marbled form from Grecian climes.

'Twere sweet to know it may be true,
  That partial friendship still may trace
Resemblances that bring to view,
  Idealized, my pictured face.

All earthly beauty fades and dies;
  Not so the beauty of the soul.
Effulgent radiance, through the eyes,
  The plainest face makes beautiful.

PLATONIC LOVE.

As plainly then so plainly now
I feel that light kiss on my brow:
    Not as one sips
    From dewy lips,

And even though the draught should bless;
'Twere wrong, he thought, thus to caress,
So he forebore; my lips he kissed them not.

So every time, from then till now,
We part, his kiss imprints my brow;
    He never yet
    The seal hath set
Upon my lips; and this but proves
He well and truly, purely, loves
Aye most sincerely loves. who wrongs me not.

But once I lifted up my lips,
As one who drinks, to cup he sips.
    But he was strong,
    And said, " 'Tis wrong."
Though lips of mine he never blessed,
Nor seal of love on them impressed,
My lips shall bless him though he kissed them not.

I'm sure, most sure, he loves me well,
Though how I know I scarce can tell;
    He told me not;
    I read (perhaps) his thought.
So better—only passion moves
The man who kneels, and swears he loves;
My true, sweet love, my own, would wrong me not.

What use for words? The birds rejoice,
And sing of love in wordless voice.
    Why plight our troth?
    Should we, when both
Do surely know what each one feels?
No honeyed words the thought conceals.
When right is his the kiss shall wrong me not.

THE HIGHEST ART.

He pictured art in Patti's song
    And argued it were vain to feel;
Emotion's throb though deep and strong
    'Twere best to stifle or conceal.

Art's realms, he said, were far above,
    And thus beyond emotion's sphere;
That highest type, artistic love,
    Did least require an object dear.

We talked in strain of pleasantness,
    As friends who differ sometimes will,
For I believed, I may confess,
    That love should own emotion's thrill.

At length we parted, as we met:
    He cold and calm, the soul of art,
While I, alas, could not forget
    Love has its birth within the heart.

That night, as on my couch I slept,
    I seemed to feel a presence near.
Some fancies o'er my senses crept—
    Some fancies which I still hold dear.

I slept, yet on my closèd eye
    Felt soft, light touch its lid impress,
As 'twere a zephyr floating by
    That lingered for this faint caress.

A moment more, warm tender lips
    Implanted on my own, a kiss
As sweet as mead the wild bee sips—
    Epitome of joyous bliss,

And this I learned that midnight hour:
  He who controls his thoughts at will,
Who feels no throb of love, hath power
  Another's inmost heart to thrill.

Thus was revealed, though in a dream,
  By phantom sign, in form of art:
The highest art is but to seem,
  And seeming love had reached my heart.

WHAT I ASK FOR.

I ASK not for riches, for riches are fleeting;
  We can buy not the joys which we sigh for in vain;
Wealth may dispel happiness, ruin completing,
  As dreams that have vanished come never again.

I ask not for honors as high as the eyrie
  Where eaglet doth hover. E'en majesty's crown
May circle a brow that is aching and weary,
  And finds no repose on a pillow of down.

I ask not for passion, its seethings alarm me,
  Though its vials be emptied and poured at my feet.
May passion's emotion of life never harm me!
  Its breath is the simoon, its storm, pelting sleet.

I ask not for fame—an ethereal vapor,
  As empty, as airy, as fleeting is fame—
A flickering light from a ha'penny taper
  Reflects but a moment, and dies with a name.

I ask not gay pleasure—a beautiful bubble,
  But hollow and fleeting, most worthless of all;
It bursts o'er one's head, making no end of trouble.
  Entice me not, pleasure, I heed not your call.

But give me contentment, whatever my station,
 Whatever my sorrow, wherever my lot,
For it casts o'er the soul rays of pure elevation,
 Though it gleam in the palace or brighten the cot.

And give me a heart full of generous feeling,
 Of kindliest love and affection for all,
With sympathy stored and its love unconcealing—
 A heart that responds to humanity's call.

And give me a mind that is strong, yet forbearing—
 As wise as a serpent, as pure as a dove;
A mind that is thoughtful, and noble, and daring,
 That soars on the pinions of heavenly love.

In this sorrowing world give me friends that are leal—
 Friends in need for my own, that are honest and true,
Through sunshine and shadow, when woe comes or weal—
 Such gifts are so rare I will ask but a few.

LINES TO A SAGE.

Now, after many years of life well spent,
Art thou serenely and in truth content?
Thou shouldst be happy, for thy fame
Has spread abroad. Is that the aim
Of happiness; or does she dwell
Unknown, in quiet, in thy breast?
Dost thou e'er suffer and yet say, " 'tis well
That I with care and grief should be oppressed?"
Is there no wish unsatisfied, no yearning quelled,
No clinging hope destroyed, no boon from thee withheld?
If thou dost dwell with love, and hope, and peace,
Ah! then, my friend, thy life is full of bliss.

In time past thou hast sorrowed; pity then
The suffering of one—that one thy friend
Till death. My path through life is rough, and when
I upward strive, I fall. Put forth thy helping hand
To guide my steps. I have no staff, no prop
On which to lean. One moment stop
And listen to my pleading. Wilt thou be
A friend in need, to counsel and encourage me,
So thy kind tones their every word shall cheer,
And bind me to thee with a tie most dear?

Few flowers, though I love flowers, brighten my path;
Few rays to light my way the sunshine hath.
The promised rainbow of my hope appears
A mockery to my eyes, flooded with tears.
A yearning, tired aching fills my breast;
Unceasing sorrow will not let me rest;
For heavy grief doth lie my heart upon.
Ah, me! yet I must bravely struggle on,
With hope, till all my earthly tasks are done—
Until I, too, the goal of peace have won.

SO WEARY.

I AM so weary, longed-for rest, the blessing
  So oft denied, I fain would sink and die,
That nightmare, care, no more should be oppressing;
  Resting upon the lap of Earth, close to her bosom lie,
    So weary now am I.

So weary, now, of fleeting joys and pleasures,
  The which, summed up, make but a paltry gain;
This cancelled by the loss of earthly treasures,
  A heavy balance leaves of aching pain.
    Weary! Ah, grieved refrain.

I am so weary! Wherefore, then, this striving
  To buffet waves that drive me evermore.
To battle with the storm, its fury still surviving,
  Why should I try, with but a single oar,
    When all is dark before?

So dark! No star of hope the night adorning,
  No hazy tint to usher in the light;
How long, O Lord, how long ere dawns the morning
  That makes the voyage of life more bright,
    Ere fades the weary night?

Hast seen a wounded bird, in struggles wasting
  The little strength it had, then, trembling, lie
With pinions broken, while, its death-throe hasting,
  It vainly flutters till it falls to die?—
    A wounded bird am I.

AN ADDRESS

TO THE BODY OF A MAN IN THE WHIRLPOOL—NIAGARA.

Ah, how ceaseless the rounds which, in darkness and gloom,
Thou hast made in the noisy confines of thy tomb,
    Since the whirlpool so great,
    Like a maelstrom of fate,
    Did fiercely surround thee.
    Drew downward and drowned thee.
    Thou shrieked but none heard thee.
    It beat thee and stirred thee,
    Despoiled thee of breath,
    And whirled thee to death.
Rising up, sinking down, with a thundering sound,
Thou art lashed by its fury around and around.
    Now to sight thou art lost;
    Like a bubble art tossed
    By the torrent's strong clasp,
    By the raging wave's grasp,

Ever round and around,
Whilst the thundering sound
Ringeth still on deaf ears,
As it did ere you drowned.
Who, alas, were thy friends who must mourn thy sad fate?
And how many are made, by thy death, desolate?
Idle questions we ask, for we never shall know
Who was tossed by these waves, or in depths thrust below,
Now so fast and now slow,
As the wild gleaming whirlpool compels thee to go;
Now a hand, or a foot
Close incased in a boot,
But a glimpse of a face—
So quickly it vanished—all too quickly to trace
Or to search out its features. Oh, terrible jest!
It is said, after death, that the body finds rest;
Finds rest! Seest thou thine? It is whirling about
From the great seething caldron no more to get out.
Didst e'er fancy a fate like to this—that thou must
Be beaten and pounded, as 'twere hastened to dust,
With a din and a roar
Like the cannon's outpour?
For an instant didst think,
As thou stoodst on the brink
And looked on the rapids, that whene'er thou wert dead
They would grind thee to dust for Niagara's bed?
For it will not be long
Ere the eddying throng—
Waves we read of in story and picture in song—
Fiercely dash thee to pieces with shriek or deep groan—
Even droppings of water will wear away stone—
They will rend thy limp limbs, and will tear them apart;
Will reach to thy vitals; they will pluck out thy heart,
Until no one can see
What resemblance there be
Or a vestige in thee
Of a being who once was a mortal like me!

A SOUVENIR.

(INSCRIBED TO HENRY W. LONGFELLOW.)

No more are the leaves of the lilac stirred,
   Where warbled in Summer the thrush ;
Nor an echo of carolling song is heard—
   Doth haunt it a mystical hush.

I seemingly see its fair blossoms lean
   O'er the porch looking into thy room,
To lovingly hallow thy thought, I ween,
   And gladden with subtle perfume.

Thy thought! doth it wander away like mine,
   E'er seeking expression in vain ;
In fancy's wreathings of imagery twine,
   Yet ever unuttered remain ?

But say ! is the elm looming stark and bare
   With foliage yellow and sear ?
Have robins departed, that nestled there,
   From landscape clouded and drear ?

Is nature attired in queenliest hue,
   Whose tints are so gorgeous and rare,
When frost has succeeded the genial dew
   And autumn wind swayeth the air ?

Pray hasten, dear poet, if not too late,
   Ere flowers and leaflets are gone,
And garner the tablet for which I wait
   Thy dear eye hath lingered upon.

A leaf or a bud that hath been caressed
   By zephyrs that hover near thee ;
Whose stem by thy hand hath been clasped and pressed,
   Pray send that memento to me.

My muse shall then soar in a wider range
  Above the pale lilac and elm ;
Be lifted where never the seasons change
  To beautiful ideal realm—

The realm where thy fancy doth float and sing
  Unmarred by the breath of a sigh ;
The poet's heart is the Eden of Spring
  Where flowers bloom brightly for aye.

Thy thought and the leaf with its net-work lines
  Are writ in symbolical lore,
My soul shall interpret the mystic signs
  My thought speak to thine evermore.

MONODY.

HE is dead! He is dead!
Ah! the words sink like lead,
  With a vibrating thud,
Far down in the heart's deepest well ;
'Tis the funeral knell
Of fond hopes. Who can tell
What an anguish profound
Ever comes, sorrow-crowned,
To the heart and the brain
Which re-echo again
  The words, He is dead! he is dead!

With a lingering refrain
Of the deepest and saddest pain,
Re-echo the words, He is dead,
The heart is so weighted,
With heavy grief freighted,

8

It will never rebound
From burden of sorrow profound.
Hark! the funeral knell
In the tones of the bell—
Waves of sound, how they swell!
How they rise, how they roll,
Like despair o'er the soul!

He is dead!   He is dead!
His soul unfettered hath fled;
'Twas this that the tolling bell said.
The requiem it sings
In my mind ever rings;
To my sad soul it brings
The words and the thought, **He** is dead!
And the slow tolling bell
And the funeral tread
Keep time to the words. He is dead;
Evermore, beating time
To the poet's sad rhyme,
On my muffled heart beating time.

A shade is over my lamp of light;
   Heavy eyelids of grief
Still press down o'er my sight.
   Sorrow brings no relief.
   Her dark clouds span my life
Which the joys of the world—
Triumph's banners unfurled—
   Nor its tumult nor strife,
Naught on earth can dispel
The gloomy shadow wherein I dwell;
   For a voice in the knell
   Of the weird sounding bell
Enthralleth my soul like a spell.

HUNTING THE FOUR-LEAF CLOVER.

LOUNGING upon the emerald green
Whose slope the trees of the forest screen,
A family group are searching over
The triune leaves for the four-leaf clover.

The matron is there with silver thread
In her waving locks; fair wife, new wed,
Love lighting her eye—the babe rolling over—
All eagerly look for the four-leaf clover.

Dear Frank and Ada, and George, and May—
Thus, half as in earnest and half in play,
Like careless quest of a woodland rover,
Their search for the ever-eluding clover.

The father looks smilingly on the scene
Nor recks if the leaflets are found, I ween;
His thoughtful care is hovering over
The loved ones lounging on bank of clover.

A bird droppeth down from its perch on high,
A butterfly aimlessly floateth by:
They too in the green and drifting over
Seem counting the leaves for four-leaf clover.

Like rarest beauties of heart and of mind,
So rare things in nature we seek to find—
Ah, loveliest spot the gaze may cover,
That vine-sheltered knoll of sweet white clover.

FAREWELL.

FAREWELL, friend, and though forever
   We may tread life's ways apart,
Time or distance ne'er can sever
   Bonds of friendship from the heart.

Wheresoe'er my footsteps linger—
   Near the vale or sounding sea,
All their beauties would be dearer,
   Fairer, friend, if shared with thee.

Nature's silent sweet communion
   Sways our thoughts with tender thrill;
And our hearts in kindred union
   Join, unmindful of our will.

Let emotion be unspoken—
   Words but hide the thought away—
Nature's silence be unbroken,
   But by zephyrs at their play.

Tender thoughts of love revealing,
   Purest joy on earth we find;
Sympathetic throbs of feeling
   Stir the heart and sway the mind.

Nature's pictures true are dearer,
   When they thrill a kindred heart;
But I may not have thee nearer,
   For our paths lie wide apart.

Farewell, friend, and should we never
   Meet again—for now we part—
May I hope that thou wilt ever
   Hold remembrance in thy heart?

DEATH'S PORTAL.

THE twilight shades are deepening into gloom;
  Smoke-wreaths, low swung, in swaying masses fall.
Undirged by tolling funeral knell, the tomb
  Of Night, Day enters, wrapped in vapory pall.

For stillness reigns. No note of wild alarm
  Disturbs the sense, nor quivers on the air,
Yet thoughts, uprising through the hushèd charm,
  Are pure hearts' vespers floating free and fair.

So stealthy shadows compass life about—
  Darken and deepen and around us fall;
As heavy clouds of grief and fear and doubt
  Would fold our being in death's funeral pall.

But all in vain. The spirit soars above
  The hovering clouds beyond the tomb, like night,
To heavenly realms. On high the God of love
  Casts o'er the soul a quenchless radiance bright.

CHURCH DEDICATION HYMN.

(*Tune,* "Maid of Athens.")

IN this, the temple of thy word
We meet to sing thy praises, Lord.
Like manna to the penitent
Thy gracious promises are sent.
Guide us aright, make clear our sight,
Oh, Lord of mercy, Lord of love!
  Look down from Heaven above.

Keep us in straight and narrow way.
Oh, never may our footsteps stray.
Teach us to do Thy holy will;
Help us Thy mandates to fulfil.
Incline Thine ear, oh, deign to hear!
And from Thy sacred throne on high
    Oh, list the sinner's cry!

Redeemer, Brother, Saviour, Friend!
To Thee our grateful prayers ascend.
Be Thou with us, whate'er betide—
For us, our Saviour crucified.
Teach us, in youth, the living truth,
Then shall our ransomed souls arise,
    To dwell in Paradise.

To Thee a faltering voice we raise;
In trembling tones we sing Thy praise.
When all our earthly songs are done
We with the angels round Thy throne
Oh, Lord of love—in Heaven above,
In newer, sweeter tones may sing
    Thy praises, Heavenly King.

WOMAN'S REVERIE.

WHEN blissful moments forever have fled—
When passion has cooled and love lieth dead,
And hope's brightest rays are by clouds overcast—
We tenderly muse o'er the joys of the past.

Oh, is there, on earth, no recompense, sweet,
For sorrows that e'er on life's pathway we meet;
For the love that entwined, like a tendril, about
The heart, to be crushed by a withering doubt?

Woman's pride, like a mask, still must ever conceal
The heart-aches, that woman alone, may feel,
Only trusting that cycles of time may prove
How true was her friendship, how pure was her love.

AGONY.

WHY, I could point the place, by pain alone,
Of nerve, or bone, or joint; each one;
      Dost ask me where
      My sufferings are?
I'll tell thee, friend, without reserve:
In this whole frame, where's joint, or bone, or nerve,
      The racking pain is there!

Thus every breath engenders pain severe,
And as I lie in suffering here,
      My inmost thought,
      (Itself pain fraught)
Is, might I sleep—sleep without breath,
E'en though I knew that silent sleep were death—
      I'd rather sleep than not.

ST. PATRICK AND THE SHAMROCK.

PATRICK the Saint to Ireland came,
Preaching the power of Jesus' name;
Teaching the one Divinity
Of that most holy Trinity.

When rose a mighty Irish chief,
Like doubting Thomas, in unbelief—

Saying, " Tell us, sir, how can it be—
The three in one, and one in three ?

" Blinded to faith I must remain
Till thou canst make the mystery plain ;
And for my life I cannot see
How three be one and one be three."

An instant paused the Saint, but thought
How simple minds are simplest taught ;
Then plucked a Shamrock, " Here," said he,
" See three in one and one in three."

As he upheld the triune leaf,
Vanished the chieftain's unbelief :
For, at his feet the Shamrock, see,
Folds three in one and one in three.

The chieftain's faith grew strong ; his clan
Espoused the cause, aye, every man.
In Ireland's emblem still we see
The oneness of a Trinity.

THEY SAY THOU ART HAPPY.

THEY say thou art happy ! Little they know
What silent sorrow, what unuttered woe,
May burden thy heart that sinketh in grief,
And seemeth no power can bring thee relief.

That yearnful longing, that nameless unrest,
Like bending head, hopeless waits to be blest ;
The heart shall find rest beyond the blue sky ;
Thy longing shall reach it, perhaps, by and by.

A peal of laughter as merry words flow
Is surface, that hides grief hidden below;
The careless tone which to jesting we lend
Is froth, cast aside, when greeting a friend.

So revelry, mirth, the cares of the world,
Or warfare of life, where flags are unfurled,
But hide sad heart-aches, and deaden the tone
Of inward sorrow, and silence its moan.

Thy heart seemeth lightsome and glad each day,
And revels in mirth, as lambkins at play;
Yet they who know grief its wailing have heard,
Like sad complaining of lone mourning bird.

A well-spring lies hidden in every heart;
At sympathy's touch its clear waters start;
Its depth is most pearly; with tear-drops fraught,
That flow from the fountains of loving thought.

By pain, and anguish we bravely endure;
The heart almost riven, is tried and made pure.
Thou reapest reward through wearisome years,
And harvest sweet thought where ye sowed but tears.

And hopes spring up when ye thought all had died—
Christ rose in glory though first crucified;
Thy thoughts send upward, thy heart bid rejoice;
There love finds expression, longing a voice.

Great trials ennoble, ingratitude smarts,
But makes us more prize the true loyal hearts.
The purest heart-throb we, stifling, conceal,
For love's full tenderness few know or feel.

They say thou'rt happy as butterfly bright,
And seemingly thoughtless of time's wingèd flight;
Should care come and heart-aches (Heaven forefend!),
And thou need sympathy, seek thou—
Thy friend.

Log cabins soon were reared by hand of arduous toil,
And with rude implements the settlers turned the soil.

THE PIONEERS.

Now fifty years agone, when these fair States were new,
Where mighty cities stand, then trackless forests grew.
Within whose dark recesses, mysterious and lone,
The winds swept sighingly with many a plaintive moan,
While mingling with the laughing, lisping waterfall
Was heard in stilly night the treacherous wild-cat's call;
Or on the startled air was borne the night-hawk's cry,
And Reynard, crouching, crept so noiselessly and sly.
Here snowy ospreys hovered, stately herons flew,
Or jay bird flitted past in coat of white and blue,
While echoed in the green secluded mossy vale
In plaintive piping notes the whippoorwill's sad wail.
With flapping pinions of the startled water-fowl
To whit! to whoo! weird cry of wise-faced solemn owl.
Then scores of wild beasts through the wooded thicket prowled
And, wolves in forest ambush sneaking, fiercely howled.

Here then did snowy swans upon the waters float,
And red men ventured forth in fragile birch-bark boat.
Onward to find the sea the winding river swept,
Above whose shaded banks the drooping willow wept,
Or dipped so lovingly beneath pellucid wave,
Its nodding plumes caressed by rippling limpid lave.
Currents unchecked flowed on or noisily or calm,
Unbridged as well, save where the beaver built his dam.
Here came in droves, to drink the waters crystal clear,
In single file, the red, and graceful fallow deer ;
Their deep sequestered paths no white man's foot had trod,
Nor o'er the vernal vales, nor meadow's unturned sod.
The whiz of pheasant's wings was heard at dewy morn
And whistling call of quail as shrill as bugle horn.
The birds sent carols forth from leafy covert gained,
While o'er the prairies vast the huge wild bison reigned.
Where now in plain and dell the herdsman's cattle roam,
Then high on rocky cliff the eagle built his home.
Log cabins soon were reared by hand of arduous toil,
And with rude implements the settler turned the soil.
Then colonies were formed, and lusty pioneer
Sustained each weary heart with words of lofty cheer.
Strong armed, with willing hand he helps the land to clear.
The hunter's rifle rang, sounded the woodman's axe,
And patient mules brought stores laden with heavy packs.
At last in beauty waved, in sheen of morning haze,
The farmer's hoard of wealth, the green and golden maize.
The water-wheel at play near swift fall of the stream
Soon churned and whirled the waves to froth and sparkling gleam,
That fell in scattered sprays from gleaming wheel's great round,
And thus the logs were sawed and farmer's grists were ground.
The great wheel drove the saw, by line, the timbers through ;
Grinding the golden grain it turned the millstone too.
And thus we backward glance at these old settlers, when
Came on that early scene the men who wield the pen.
All honor to those men, the bravest heroes known.
The moving force were they, the power behind the throne.

The valiant knights of type and gray goose quill were they,
Who through the forests lone for homes did blaze the way.
They came enlightening, to civilize and bless,
With strong compelling force, the hand-run printing-press.
Where erst had only been the thicket's tangled wood,
By labor's sure reward the church and school-house stood.
These changes wrought by hand of rugged pioneers
When our great peopled States were termed " the west frontiers."

SHADOWS.

O'ER every home some shadows fall,
Yet heaven's sunlight shines for all.
To every life come clouds like night,
And yet beyond them beams the light.

Our fairest dreams are ne'er fulfilled ;
Hope's budding flowers rude frosts have chilled ;
Thus comes to all, or soon or late,
Experience dark of adverse fate.

They seem as clouds that dim life's sky,
Yet are but shadows flitting by,
Born of soft sunlight's ray serene,
And passing mists that intervene—

Shadows, not clouds, that light and shade,
With shimmering touch, each grassy blade ;
That come and go and still allure,
And chase each other o'er the moor.

Shadows that come from sunset beam,
To some as darkest clouds must seem.
Look not too low, lift up thine eyes,
See, far above are cloudless skies,

While love and hope, and faith supreme,
Make darkest clouds as shadows seem.
At hide-and-seek they idly play,
And touch the heart, then flit away.

A MOTHER'S ANGUISH.

Oh, Myla, my darling,
My sunbeam, my starling!
My birdling has flitted, my darling is gone.
Oh, why didst thou leave me?
Or why shouldst thou grieve me?
My darling, my precious, why leave me alone?

She the tendril, close winding,
The love, my heart binding,
Has left it all bleeding, when torn from my side,
And my poor heart is grieving,
In sorrow bereaving,
Oh, why has she left me, my precious, my pride?

E'en though I be sinning
By ceaseless complaining,
The Lord will forgive, for my poor brain is wild.
Though the anguish I'm stilling,
I cannot be willing
To be severed fore'er from my darling, my child.

My heart, torn and bleeding,
Dear Father, is pleading,
I am lonely! so lonely; most saddening moan,
Its sorrow bereaving,
List to the heart grieving,
Oh, give back my darling, nor leave me alone!
*   *   *   *   *   *   *   *   *

I thank thee this even,
  Oh Father in Heaven ;
'Twas a horrible dream. My darling is here,
    With her smiles and caressing,
    Close to my heart pressing ;
Oh Father, I thank thee, I bless thee fore'er.

    So real the seeming
      Of death, in my dreaming,
Though gone is the dream, and unbroken our band,
    Yet a moral 'tis teaching,
    So many hearts reaching :
Thank God all the while for the gifts from his hand.

THE POET.

FRATERNALLY INSCRIBED TO J. W. R.

WHO shall depicture the passionate pain
  That dwells in the poet's soul ;
Throbbing and surging like wave of the main,
  Leaping beyond all control ?

Thrilled by a thought-germ, stirred by a breath,
  Filled with emotions his breast ;
Suffering, longing, and hoping till death
  Bringeth a surcease and rest.

Praying for something—a look or a word ;
  Breathing a sigh or a moan ;
Listening as one who in music hath heard
  The depth of its sad undertone.

Poet, thy spirit is held by a spell,
  Wrapped in the mist of a dream ;
No outlet hath language thy fancies to tell,
  Though they so real do seem.

Could I say something sad hearts to relieve—
 Wake the soul-echoes of song—
In beautiful garlands of thought would I weave
 Words lying silent so long.

Kindliest wishes with love all aglow,
 Enwreathing the hope I twine,
That never another's spirit may know
 The sadness that shadoweth mine.

LOVE'S PLEADING.

THINK of me, darling; of thee am I thinking,
 Ever and always most fondly of thee.
Drink to me, darling, the nectar I'm drinking—
 Drink of the cup that brings sweetness to me.

Dream of me, darling; of thee am I dreaming,
 Day-time and night-time and all of the time.
Purest of pleasure is ever in seeming—
 Dreams may come true in a happier clime.

Pray for me, darling; for thee am I praying;
 May all earthly blessings be showered on thee;
Refreshing as fountain, whose waters are playing,
 Thy fount or thy well-spring of joy will I be.

Love me, oh, darling! for thee am I loving;
 'Tis joy fraught with grief, and bliss thrilled with pain.
Tell me you love me, my love still approving.
 I never can doubt it! yet tell me again.

Cling to me, darling; to thee am I clinging.
 Be strong to sustain me, I'm only a vine,
Yet a beautiful grace and fragrance I'm bringing.
 Ah! close round thy heart let my tendrils entwine.

Fly to me, darling; to thee am I flying;
  In spirit I come, for my spirit is thine.
List to its longing that breathes forth in sighing,
  An ecstasy sweet, that is thine, love, and mine.

THE DYING CHILD.

The wintry winds without were sighing;
Within a lovely child lay dying;
Death hastes, on wingèd moments flying—
Her eyes half closed 'neath fringèd veil,
Resting on cheeks as lily pale.

The quickened pulse, her grasping breath,
As plain as any language saith
She soon, too soon, must yield to death.
Nerveless and white the tiny hand,
'Erst like the shell from India's strand.

But see! the color mounts the cheek;
The filmy eyes the mother's seek;
The pallid lips essay to speak;
A joyous light beams from the eyes—
A glorious dawn of pleased surprise.

No look of sorrow, pain, or fear—
Breathless, the watchers gather near;
Bend o'er the child, her parents dear—
With hand uplifted o'er her head,
"See, mamma, see!" the dear one said.

Came from her lips no other word;
Silent she lay, nor moved nor stirred.
Grief's broken sobs alone were heard.
Had God endowed those dying eyes
With power to see beyond the skies?

"See, mamma, see!" Yet how can we—
So earthly still—how can it be
That we, with purblind sight, should see
The scene that gladdened dying eyes,
That seemed a glimpse of Paradise?

"See, mamma, see!" Through earthly throes
Her eyes are beaming, ere they close
In that long-lasting, sweet repose
Of death. Perhaps the angel band
Had clasped the child's uplifted hand.

And then she smiled nor longed to stay,
But with those angels passed away,
Through realms of night to realms of day.
"See, mamma, see!" 'twas all she said,
And soon the darling child was dead.

"See, mamma, see!" with fond regret
Enshrined in memory linger yet;
Life's parting words we ne'er forget.
Ah, may they lift our longing eyes
Till we, too, see beyond the skies.

PROPHET AND MOUNTAIN.

THE truth I will seek in a query,
  While I gaze in the depths of thine eyes.
Think'st thou that Mahomet was very
  Remarkably, wondrously wise?

A journey he took to a mountain,
  Perchance there to breathe out his sighs,
Like bubbles thrown off by the fountain;
  Yet, say, does that prove he was wise?

I ask you in all truth and candor—
    For falsehood's a cheat I despise—
Though he to the mountain would wander,
    In that can you think he was wise?

The mountain would come to him never—
    At least so methinks some one cries—
Though he longed and yearned for it ever,
    So, perhaps, in truth he was wise.

You and I, to strengthen my meaning,
    May the mount and prophet comprise;
Though one to the other is leaning,
    Yet, say, can you think it is wise?

To the mount the prophet draws nearer;
    It may not occasion surprise
Should each to the other grow dearer,
    Yet, I fear it cannot be wise.

The mountain is reached, and together
    Their brows they uplift to the skies,
Communing with Nature—but whether,
    Say, whether *our* prophet is wise?

THE BROTHERHOOD OF MAN.

DEDICATED TO T. W. H.

In centuries long gone, poet and sage began
To teach a noble lesson, the brotherhood of Man.
As each one learned and passed away, his life a stepping-stone
Became, and thus they reach from that day to our own.

And flights of time present, by circling cycles spanned,
A stairway broad, upreaching, high and grand,
Fair, strong, enduring, inspiring e'en to see—
Its basis firm, unfailing—the rock of charity.

On this foundation rises superstructure fair to see,
Supported on the pillars of a broad humanity;
Its halls and arches beautiful, whose gildings ne'er grow dim,
Its domes and spires reach heavenward, point ever up to Him

Who glorifies the spirit that soars beyond the skies;
Who teaches thought expression, as its longings upward rise,
To the tessellated terrace where the sunshine smiles to see
The gilder's burnished halo, on the walls of porphyry.

The ambient air is warm and pure; religion hath no need
To cloak in garb of hypocrite to save her sons by creed.
Her code is in her pillars grand of broad humanity,
Her creed on her foundation-stone, the mystic lore of Charity.

WAITING.

WAITING for thought-buds to spring at my bidding,
 To blossom in beautiful flowers of rhyme;
  Though beauty enchanting
  Is lost by transplanting
 From the mind to this page, far more rigorous clime.

Waiting for visions that live in my mem'ry
 To step from their prison, stand fair to the view,
  And tell the brave story,
  How one mortal's glory
 Was to ever be hopeful and loving and true.

Waiting for one who to me should be hast'ning;
  Waiting and watching and hoping again.
    Ah! sure, did he love me,
    He would not thus prove me.
  But alas, weary heart, thou art waiting in vain!

Waiting for trials and storms that come sweeping;
  Life's trials and sorrows, like thickening gloom,
    Aye, gather around us,
    And grieve us and wound us.
  Till our only escape seems a welcoming tomb.

EOLIA'S HARP.

EOLIA's harp is like my heart,
  And thou art like the passing wind;
Whose touch with wondrous, magic art,
  Brings forth a language undefined.

The pallid flower grows yet more pale,
  Swept by the chilling breath of frost,
The human heart sends forth a wail
  When cynic hand its chords hath crossed.

Thy loving glance doth send a thrill
  My being through, while at thy word
My trembling heart-chords vibrate, till,
  To rhythmic rune, my thoughts are stirred.

'Tis thou dost give the harp its tone,
  Entrancing winged, aerial thought;
Its tender, weird, or plaintive moan—
  Its fancies bright from thee are caught.

Breathe gently o'er my heart, oh wind,
  With fond caress, as lovers woo;
Its music—language undefined—
  Its sleeping tones awake for you.

Blow softly o'er Æolian string,
  As 'neath the blue the zephyr flies.
If love be borne upon thy wing
  The harp responds in dulcet sighs.

Then stir with not too dalliant touch,
  Æolian harp of human kind,
Nor strain its tension overmuch
  To shatter heart-strings, careless wind.

Oh wanton wind, breath of my fate,
  A woman's heart is swayed by thee.
Swept rudely thou wilt find too late
  Its broken chords hang silently.

LIFE'S UNDERTONE.

Surging are the waves of feeling
  Rising from the restless soul,
Yearning, throbbing thoughts revealing—
  Waves that brook of no control.

Yet doth strong and still emotion
  Greater depth of feeling show;
As in quiet deeps of ocean
  Silently the currents flow.

Flowing lines with beauty glowing
  Hide ofttimes an undertone;
Prayers and tears swift currents flowing
  Till they reach to Heaven's zone.

Tender thoughts are currents blending;
　Joy beneath a sigh oft glows.
Love, the deepest, is unending
　As eternity's repose.

————　··

THE BIRD AND FLOWER.

On tree-top sways the singing bird
　That charms the sense from day to day;
Yet, captured, caged, no more is heard,
　In gladsome song, its thrilling lay.

Unnoticed, blooms the way-side flower
　That blesses with its sunlit eyes,
Yet, rudely plucked in luckless hour,
　It fades; in fainting fragrance dies.

No gilded cage that wealth can buy
　So dear to me as wildwood tree;
No shelter like the brooding sky;
　With joy to sing I must be free.

I'd rather be the simple flower
　That cheers the weary passer-by,
Than rose that brightens beauty's bower,
　Though unadmired I bloom and die.

I would be like the flower and bird—
　The flower unplucked, the birdling free—
With bloom to bless, whose notes are heard
　In chords that thrill with sympathy.

AN ECHO.

MORE swift than the barque speeding over the ocean,
  More fair than the sail floating on to the lee,
Is the thought-bird that dips in the fount of emotion
  And soars on invisible pinions to me.

It wakens a presence that lightly was sleeping
  In magical palace so wondrously wrought;
Where Memory ever her vigil is keeping,
  This presence responds to the love-laden thought.

A whisper as noiseless as dew fall, distilling
  Its life-giving sweets o'er each flower and knoll.
So still is the echo whose presence, whilst thrilling
  Each nerve of the heart, still enraptures the soul.

An echo that answers sweet thought-wafted wishes,
  An echo repeating the heart's hidden lore,
That revels in longings and ecstatic blisses;
  From Memory's realm it replies evermore.

LONGINGS.

Is sadness but love's completeness?
  Joy ever alloyed with fears?
Doth time prove only the fleetness
  Of the passage of wingèd years?

Is life to be clouded with sorrow
  'Till earth seems a night-shrouded plain?
Doth hope falsely whisper, to-morrow
  May bring thee a surcease from pain?

Are pleasure and mirth and gladness
　　All joys that the world can bring?
Must envy and malice and sadness
　　Wound the heart as with poisonous sting?

There's a depth of yearning and longing
　　Expressed in the half-uttered sigh,
And turbulent thoughts that come thronging,
　　As though they would speak from the eye.

Though ye grieve with the soul sadly aching,
　　Rejoice in its happy release,
For ye know that a heart that is breaking,
　　May soon find the solace of peace.

No happiness e'er in the throbbing
　　Of the unquiet bosom there dwells,
But a wail comes forth in its sobbing
　　That rises and surges and swells.

But cometh a peace most enduring,
　　When the tumult termed life shall have ceased,
And the spirit slips forth from its mooring,
　　The soul is from durance released.

IN STARLIT HEIGHTS.

IN starlit heights I sit, and look below.
I see the worldlings pass like crawling snails—
The myriads wrestling tremulous and weak
Like puny worms tangled in writhing mass.
And thus I view them from so far away—
From reaches, infinite, of azure sea—
Perpetual calm unmarred by discord's strife.
My earthly semblance seemeth there to be,

Yet on this burnished cloud, enthroned, sit I,
And float in peaceful calm above the earth,
Serenely smiling o'er the trivial aims,
The efforts, purposeless, of worldly wise.
So! let them think me there, the while
My spirit soars through boundless depths aloft.
Illumined, in the vast expanse of Heaven,
It spans the universe, and rising o'er,
Greeteth its glorious maker—God.

THE POET'S SONG.

TO THE AUTHOR OF "LAURA, MY DARLING."

THE swift emotions of my soul
  Still rise and surge and throng,
At length, burst free from all control,
  They swell the stream of song.

Let sympathy for human love,
  With grief for every wrong,
Be as the waves that lift above
  And bear the strain along.

Let love and truth and kindly thought
  Impel the current strong,
Till inspiration true is caught
  Upon the wave of song.

OUT OF THE DEPTHS.

SILENT and still my depth of grief to-night
  Unfathomed lies, beneath a surface fair,
Whereon no ripple plays; wherein no light
  Reflects; where'er are hovering clouds of care.

My wounded heart like sea-wreck, idly drifts
   Dismantled, at the mercy of the wind-swept tides;
Or erst is borne on rolling sea that lifts
   To plunge it deeper 'neath the wave it rides.

If that I knew no other heart to-night
   Were sunk in grief, or surging with a moan,
My darkened path, methinks, would seem more bright—
   If others walked with joy, with sorrow I alone.

Alas, alas!—If I alone might bear
   The grief of all, the wearying toil and strife,
Then I content would lift the weight of care,
   Bring Hope's fair sunlight to each shadowed life.

IN MEMORIAM.

I AM sitting beside thy grave, darling,
   'Neath trees near its grassy green mound;
The murmuring breeze through the leaves, darling,
   Wakes my heart to responsive resound.

In spirit you whisper to me, darling,
   And beckon me ever to come;
And footprints of time on life's path, darling,
   Lead on to a heavenly home.

When followed my life's darkest night, darling,
   With never a starlight's faint gleam,
I could not arouse from the thrall, darling,
   Seeming so like a horrible dream.

Many years have gone by since then, darling,
   And sorrows passed over my head,
Since I took up life's burden again, darling,
   With hope, not unmingled with dread.

I linger again in the past, darling,
  'Midst pleasures and scenes long agone,
Ere Fate's ruthless hand struck the blow, darling,
  That left me to struggle alone.

With death's icy chill on your brow, darling,
  When rebellious my heart was, you said,
"'Tis His will; He knows best." Oh, my darling!
  Yet thou liest low with the dead.

But "He knoweth best," so you said, darling,
  I bowed to the chastening rod ;
Were't not for our pledges of love, darling,
  I, too, would have slept 'neath the sod.

But life had a duty for me, darling,
  'Tis the walk to the distaff I tread ;
In path of a duty to do, darling,
  Reweaving my life's broken thread.

SORROW'S CLOUDS.

(A Hymn.)

When sorrow's clouds my life o'ercast,
  And shades of night encompass me ;
When storms of grief are gathering fast,
  I'll fly for refuge, Lord, to thee.

My weary heart and yearning soul,
  My blinded eyes that long to see ;
That seek to find the heavenly goal,
  I bring them all, O Lord, to thee.

The faltering faith that should believe,
  The evil thoughts that dwell with me;
The sinful heart wilt thou receive?
  My burdens, Lord, I bring to thee.

Restore a faith that will abide,
  And purer thoughts give unto me:
Take from my heart its sinful pride.
  Exalt my soul that cries to thee.

TIME'S FLIGHT.

A CHILD is born of agonizing pain—
Another ripple scarce disturbs the main;
Another foot essays life's hill to climb,
Yet leaves no footprint on the sands of time.

Time flying past on swift, propelling wings,
The future promises the present brings;
The present, see it fall, the feathered quill,
The which we catch, and quickly point, at will,

The feathered tip that from Time's pinion fell;
This is the present—now the future tell.
The past is gone; wafted too near the shore,
'Twas washed away; 'tis gone for evermore.

The past is gone, the faint receding wave,
Bore that away to find a watery grave;
The future, though Time promise fair and fine,
Hope's buoyant plume may ne'er on earth be thine.

Grasp then the present, let this priceless pen
Inscribe kind thoughts, record good deeds of men;
Time's gift to thee, shall write upon Time's wall:
Lose not the present else thou losest all.

The sloping banks, the bonny braes.
The trance of Nature's hush.

POET AND ARTIST.

A THOUGHT goes flitting through the mind
　　That scarce can be expressed,
Floating so lightly, unconfined,
　　Dear fancy's wingèd guest.

Emotions rise like waters still,
   Encompassing the heart—
To limn invites the artist skill,
   Inspires poetic art.

The sloping banks, the bonny braes,
   The trance of Nature's hush,
Call forth the poet's roundelays,
   The artist's magic brush;

And every soulful act of grace,
   Emotions strong and deep,
That light with joy the sunny face—
   Drooped eyelids tears o'erleap.

The undulating hills, the dale,
   In Nature's garb enshrined,
Reflected are in image pale
   On poet-artist mind.

So Poetry and Art must be
   United evermore;
In Nature's realm, o'er land or sea,
   All mysteries they explore.

And each shall strive and strive again
   With emulative art,
With inspiration's brush and pen
   Pure pleasures to impart;

While love, and hope, and faith sublime,
   And heavenly rapture sweet—
Upborne by lifted waves of time,
   Earth's gifted children greet.

A POET'S WHISPERED ROUNDELAY.*

WHAT may I bring—what blessing rare,
  To crown with joy thy natal day?
An incense wafted on the air—
  A poet's whispered roundelay.

Dear friend, as fails the limner's art
  To catch the impress of the mind—
To picture forth the noble heart
  That throbs with love for all mankind—

So language never can express
  The reverence and emotion deep,
The breadth and depth of tenderness—
  Of thoughts that birthday vigils keep.

Thou lifter-up of those oppressed,
  And brave defender of the weak,
Humanity has made thee blest—
  Can I thy praises truly speak?

Nay; only do I bring the meed
  Of sympathy—small tribute mine;
And yet all whiles we must have need
  Of human comfort and divine.

Dear friend, long may'st thou linger here
  To bless the poor who love thy name,
And when thou'rt gone each passing year
  Revive thy memory and thy fame.

---

* To Hon. Horace P. Biddle, on his seventieth birthday, March 24, 1881.

TO MYLA.

LITTLE daughter, precious child,
Lift thy soulful eyes so mild,
While I tell thee what I bring
For a birthday offering.

Prize it, then, all else above—
Priceless gift is mother-love,
Shielding thee from care and strife—
Mother loves thee more than life.

Ten winged years have o'er thee flown;
Soon thou'lt be to woman grown.
Years are leaves that, one by one
The rose unfolds, till fully blown.

Silent prayers for thee I breathe,
Hope's fair flowers for thee I wreathe;
Prayers and hopes, from day to day,
Send I forth to guard thy way.

Be thou ever pure and fair
As unfolding rosebuds rare;
Scatter kindness, e'en as they
Shed a fragrance o'er the way.

May good deeds, from opening morn
Till its close, thy life adorn;
Be thou fresh and sweet and true,
A flower baptized in heaven's dew.

As fair as the soft eider down
Are the ringlets that form her rich crown.

GARDINA.

I KNOW of a monarch most queenly,
Who governs her subjects serenely—
In a pretty, imperious way,
Ruling all who come under her sway.
Her title is perfect, I ween, a
Most royal, most regal—Gardina;
    Her Highness, Our Baby, Gardina.

There are sprites, by the legion, that rise,
And sparkle and dance in her eyes;
As fair as the soft eider-down
Are the ringlets that form her rich crown;
In color just something between a
Snow-flake and sunbeam, o'er Gardina;
    Her Highness, Our Baby, Gardina.

Her footbeats thrill hearts with delight
As they patter from morning till night;
Her devoted adherents at hand,
Obey her least sign of command;
I doubt if there be so serene a
Sweet tyrant as little Gardina;
    Her Highness, Our Baby, Gardina.

Mother, father, and brothers obey,
Uncles, cousins, and aunts own her sway,
Her rule—let it be understood—
Extends o'er the whole neighborhood;—
But perhaps you may know or have seen a
Rare, beautiful Queen, like Gardina;
    Her Highness, Our Baby, Gardina.

SOLILOQUY.

WHY, when I seek to float on wings of fancy,
To realms of imagery, in high-flown course;
To dreaming lie upon the mountain-tops
Of Reverie sweet; or, soaring upward,
Reach to the highest pinnacle of thought—
Why is it that, when thus I long to fly,
My wings refuse to lift and bear me up?
And courage fails, and fear still drags me down,
And will not let me rise; and I must needs
Grow timid—scarce will try the flight nor use
The pinions Nature hath provided me?
What, then, wouldst have me do—what course pursue?
Must I, then, train these spreading wings of thought,
To strengthen them, that they may bear me up,
And bravely heavenward; or clip them close,
And ever be content, like barnyard fowl,
Or eaglet of its pinions shorn, to hover near the ground?
May I not bathe these wings, to start their growth,
In limpid streams of Poesy—nor yet
Approach those famous rivers, Rhyme and Reason—
Nor tempt my timid muse to sound their praises?

DESERTED.

You have crushed my heart as in iron vise;
   You have trampled it under your feet,
And my tears burn dry ere I let them rise
   To prove that you triumph complete.

Whatever is sad as a woman's love,
   So sad, yet how wondrously sweet!
Tender as tremulous coo of the dove,
   Its gift, abnegation complete.

Ye reck not its worth, but laughingly sneer
   At grieving and womanly dread;
That you may be false, your love insincere,
   Or breathed to another instead.

I sit in the gloaming and silently muse
   O'er joys of the unwritten past,
And wake to the thought that to love is to lose,
   And dream-life hath vanished at last.

Seeking fairer delights you waywardly roam;
   I mourn your departure alone.
I grieve that my heart is no longer your home—
   That you are no longer my own.

THE MAGI-MINSTREL.

TALES are told of minnesingers in chivalrous days of yore
Who expressed their tenderest feelings, oft, in music's lyric lore;
Who ersttimes did win the loved one wealth and power had vainly
    sought,
By the whispered strains of music with devotion's spell inwrought.

I would be the minnesinger, magi-minstrel, in the guise
Of a poet, whose deep feelings in the forms of verse arise;
I would weave a spell of magic by the power love gives to me,
And the fairest thoughts and treasures tenderly I'd bring to thee.

I'd endow thee with all virtues—thought's fair blessings good
    and pure—
All the graces, highest pleasures, that ennoble and endure—
Wisdom's mantle, honor's signet, and the priceless pearls of
    truth—
Stay Time's flight and clip his pinions; give thy heart undying
    youth.

I would wreathe thy brow with laurel, and my off'ring to com-
    plete—
Forward bend thy crownèd forehead—see, my heart lies at thy
    feet,
And the longing in my bosom, as my eager eyes uplift,
Is that thou wilt cherish tenderly and prize the precious gift.

BABY.

Baby with the limpid eyes—
Azure snatched from out the skies;
In and out the sunbeams glide,
Seeking in thy curls to hide.
On thy brow, so pure and fair,
All unfraught with line of care.
Yet of thought I seem to see
Richly-freighted argosy.
On thy cheeks the sunny glint
Mingles with the roses' tint.
In thy features all, I trace
Innocence and childish grace;
While thy lips, like Cupid's bow,
Drew their form thereform, I trow,
For a Cupid folded in
Lurks in the dimple of thy chin.

SOME TIME, SOMEWHERE.

For if ye sow, with prayerful faith, the seeds—
    Let fall o'er them the tear of sympathy,
The sunshine, cheering words, which each one needs-
    Some time, somewhere, the harvest ye shall see.

Thus, they who heavenly precepts would instil,
  Must watch and pray, must early work, and late,
With faith to see, with love to do God's will.
  For them the harvest shall indeed be great.

THE DEW-DROP.

I saw a diamond glistening in the grass,
Along a path where once I chanced to pass.
It blazed with changing, scintillating light;
I knew the gem was precious, for it shone so bright.
I stood and watched its iridescent rays,
Now gold, now silver, now in purple, blaze.
Methought such bright and shimmering rays of light
Could ne'er before have gladdened mortal's sight.
To grasp the radiant gem, nearer I drew;
'Twas but a drop of dew, its glorious rays
Were Heaven's beams the sun sent shining through.

SORROW'S HARVEST.

The seeds of trouble so thickly are cast;
  Into each life they fall,
And clouds of sorrow are gathering fast,
  Yet Heaven may shelter us all.

When after the rain comes the sunlit glow,
  And white wings float o'erhead,
We look for the harvest of sorrow, but lo!
  Hath wisdom sprung up in its stead.

A VANISHED SUMMER.

You dream of a vanished summer,
  Of a lingering, sad, good-by,
You welcome with love the new-comer,
  And turn from the old with a sigh.

Your being is stirred with affection
  At touch of memory's hands;
From the grave of fond recollection
  A loved one before you stands.

You vow to be constant forever—
  To one you will always be true;
Can you look o'er the past, and say never
  Have changes been wrought out in you?

You will love me as now you are loving?
  Nay! we cannot the future foretell;
So whene'er or where'er you are roving,
  My heart-thought shall whisper, farewell.

LIFE.

Life is a toil,
Unceasing turmoil;
A hill to climb,
A rest—some time;
A battle to fight,
To dare, and do right;
A current to brave
In the seething wave,

Or outward to glide
With the ebbing tide.
'Tis a race to be run
Till the goal is won;
A bark on the wave
We must struggle to save;
A hope—only this,
A semblance of bliss;
A journey begun;
(Would the journey were done!)
A longing for love,
Its expression above;
A nameless unrest;
A wish to be blest;
A joy and a tear,
Life mingles them here;
A tortuous road
Through a tangled wood;
A lingering regret;
A grief to forget;
A ceasing from strife,
Is the ending of life.

THE FLOWER HE GAVE.

A SINGLE flower he gave to me,
  Fragrant with perfume sweet,
Whose symbol, loving thought I see—
  Perfection most complete:
And much I wondered if it seemed
  To him so fair a thing;
If 'neath my silent mien he dreamed
  Some fancies bright would spring.

Or if he knew, that, like a flower,
   A woman's love doth grow,
Expanding gently hour by hour,
   In perfect bloom to glow.
Aye, much I wondered if Love seemed
   To him so fair a thing;
Or, idly plucked, like flower, he deemed
   Its sweets aside to fling.

The flower lay on my bosom, as
   He said "fair resting-place,"
As he might think the blossom has
   Attained a subtler grace;
But ah, I wondered if it seemed
   To him, that such a thing
Would make me shrink, as though I dreamed
   His words some harm might bring.

Oh, woman's love!   Oh, flowers that blow,
   So fraught with rapture sweet;
How few the hearts that fully know
   The bliss ye bear complete!
And ah, I wondered if he dreamed
   A flower-song I would bring!
The richest gem that ever gleamed
   Is Love that poets sing.

LOVE'S TRIBUTE.

THERE is naught on earth so wondrously sweet
   As love fulfilling its mission:
Nor aught in nature so perfect, complete
   In the joy of its full fruition.

An ecstatic thrill doth glowingly flow
   Through hearts thus holding communion,
While each through self-abnegation shall know
   The bliss of a perfect union.

To feel, as the dear one encircled you hold,
   That life has no greater pleasure,
That gems unrivalled and wealth untold
   Can never purchase the treasure.

Yet language hath never the word to express
   The yearning thoughts, that come thronging
To halo the object of tenderness,
   With exquisite blissful longing.

RONDEAU.

LET us love
While we may.
Land above,
Land of clay,
Do unite
Fair and bright;
Do meet
And complete,
In unions,
Communions—
Something sweet
Which we greet;
For its form,
Mid life's storm
Gives us hope,
Lifts us up
On its wings,
Joy it brings,
And with wiles
Care beguiles.
Thus our song,
Loud and long,

E'er the same,
Bears the name
Of this dove.
Call it "Love"—
Thrills our heart,
Every part—
May it come
To its home,
Build its nest
In our breast,
We are blest—
Love possessed.

THE THOUGHT-BIRD.

SILENT, I muse in the soft, waning light,
While my hovering thought is pluming for flight;
        With deep tenderness,
        Words cannot express,
I send forth my thought-bird, far soaring to-night.

Float onward, fair thought, strong, yet airy you seem,
As feather, wind-wafted o'er fast-flowing stream;
        My love haste to bless
        With spirit caress,
Enfold him in gossamer mist of a dream.

Wingèd thought, soar away through ethery skies,
Straight home to my love, as a carrier-dove flies,
        And weave in his breast
        The downiest nest—
Find shelter fore'er 'neath the light of his eyes.

Yet stay—Thought! a gift—hide it under your wing,
All unknown to my love a heart I would bring.

When you are caressed,
My heart, too, is blessed,
Its joy-throb to smother, sweet thought-bird, you sing.

LOVE'S FOUNT.

STRAY your feet
To love's fount; may you bring
In your heart, love to me,
Nectar sweet!
Let us taste, let us sing,
As in tasting we see
Joy complete!

Do you think
Such a nectar would pall
On the taste, or the heart
Cease to drink;
All unheeding love's call,
From love's sweetness depart—
At the brink?

Can you guess?
In this fount is a spell,
For a thrill, like a tone,
Does possess
Those who drink at love's well;
Nectar sip, love's alone,
Love's caress!

Love divine
Thrills our hearts as we sip,
And we feel love possessed—
Thou art mine;
I am thine;

'Tis nectar we quaff from the lip;
  Kisses sweet, rapture blest
    With love's wine!

    Like a dove,
In the heart, perfect bliss
  Finds a home.   Swell our song
    Far above
Other songs; love's first kiss,
  Tremulous, thrilling and long,
    Kiss of love!

    Perfect bliss
In the heart, like a dove,
  Finds a home—perfect rest.
    Who would miss
    Joy like this,
Of a heart filled with love?
  Oh, the rapture expressed
    In love's kiss!

INCOMPREHENSIBLE.

UPON the porch he turned, to fling,
  From finger-tips a light caress;
How strange that such an airy thing
  Should stir the fount of tenderness!

More strange my wish that lips so sweet
  Should hunger with a fond regret;
As one whose draught is incomplete
  Yet craves the drop he failed to get.

'Twere strange indeed, and yet it seems
  As though in spirit he were here;
Yet stranger still if in his dreams
  A semblance of myself appear.

Strange as we tread life's tortuous way,
   Thrilled with love's holy tenderness,
We may not fling reserve away,
   Nor pure emotions dare express.

MY SPIRIT TURNS TO THEE.

Now let me whisper in thine ear!
   Most dear thou art to me.
In dreams I see thy form appear;
   My spirit turns to thee—
       To thee,
   My spirit turns to thee.

Thy sweetness draws me on, dear one,
   As nectar draws the bee;
As sunflower turns to greet the sun,
   My spirit turns to thee—
       To thee,
   My spirit turns to thee.

Thou art the fairest, dearest, best—
   To me shalt ever be;
I love them not, nor seek the rest—
   My spirit turns to thee—
       To thee,
   My spirit turns to thee.

Then doubt me not, nor fear to trust.
   My heart thou e'en shall see;
Look in my bosom, see thou must.
   My spirit turns to thee—
       To thee,
   My spirit turns to thee.

DISILLUSIONED.

I know not why, when men deceive
We still their false sweet words believe,
And fold delusions to the heart—
False phantoms formed by studied art.

Is nothing real?   Is nothing true?
Does all in me seem false to you?
Do you, too sadly, idly grieve
That doubt will not let you believe?

Do kindly words which you receive
Within your heart sad echoes leave?
Would all were true—faith sweep away
The clouds of life, and light its day.

The human heart sends forth a tone
When stirred by doubt, like stifled moan,
As wind-swept harp whose rhythmic rune
Sounds harsh, discordant, out of tune.

THE OFFERING.

From the world I tread a little apart,
  Through the path that leads to my king;
To him, all the wealth of my womanly heart
  Is the priceless treasure I bring.

For the casket is stored with pearls of thought,
  That grew from heart-woundings and tears,
Gathered in suffering, patiently sought
  In the sands of the by-gone years.

It holdeth a gem as a diamond bright;
    'Tis the purest of earthly love;
Lending to darkness a radiant light,
    As the stars that are beaming above.

Ah! can he reject such a peerless gift,
    Or can he my off'ring disdain?
At his feet lies the gem; the casket I lift;
    Now 'tis heavy with aching pain.

SWEET WISHES.

Softly stirred is womanly duty
    To what I should do for my love.
I would halo his life with a beauty
    As fair as the heavens above.

I'd enfold him in tender caressings,
    And pillow his head on my breast:
I would shower the choicest of blessings
    On the brow where my lips should be pressed.

I would mingle the sound of sweet kisses
    With chords of the poet's own lyre;
Enrich him with warm, glowing blisses
    Which genius hath welded with fire.

Entangled in Cupid's strong meshes,
    My faith, love, and duty are blent,
Whence I waft him a breath of sweet wishes:
    In rhythmical rune they are sent.

DARLING, THINK OF ME.

WHEN pleasure crowns thy pathway
  As sunset crowns the sea,
And all is joy and gladness,   .
  Then, darling, think of me.

In vista of the future,
  When promise rich thou'lt see,
Still in that hour remember,
  And, darling, think of me.

Should days of gloomy sorrow
  Their shadows cast o'er thee,
Yet, even then, remember,
  And sometimes think of me.

If in thy heart a yearning
  For kindred sympathy,
Should swell that heart to bursting,
  My darling, think of me.

And oh, may all the brightness
  Of love, be cast o'er thee;
Yet in thy love's fruition
  Sometimes you'll think of me.

For all must have their sorrows—
  A few may happy be;
So then, in joy or sadness,
  Think kindly still of me.

In memory then will linger—
  Aye, linger lovingly—
In my heart thoughts of you, love,
  In your heart thoughts of me.

HAPPY TO-NIGHT.

You have tenderly, fondly caressed me,
   And folded me near to your heart ;
With a kiss on my brow you have blessed me,
   And that blessing shall never depart.
      Oh, yes, I am happy to-night, darling,
       Happy, so happy to-night.

I have lifted my head from your shoulder
   As a footstep hath caused me alarms,
Whilst you, through love's loyalty, bolder,
   Enwrapped me more close in your arms.
      Oh, yes, I am happy to-night, darling,
       Happy, so happy to-night.

I have read in your eyes a sweet story
   By the love-light that flashed from my own,
And Cupid now halos with glory
   Life's path I had traversed alone.
      Oh, yes, I am happy to-night, darling,
       Happy, so happy to-night.

I have felt the warm throb of emotion
   Respondent to loving caress ;
I have dreamed that a world of devotion
   My being may brighten and bless.
      Oh, yes, I am happy to-night, darling,
       Happy, most happy to-night.

How blissful the moments, though fleeting,
   Of pleasure unmixed with alloy,
When souls are in ecstasy meeting
   And hearts are vibrating with joy !
      Oh, yes, I am happy to night, darling,
       Happy, so happy to-night.

Whatever the future is bringing,
  Or Time bears away in its flight,
A bird in my bosom is singing
  Because I am happy to-night.
      Oh, yes, I am happy to-night, darling,
        Happy, so happy to-night.

THE OAK AND THE VINE.

AH, yes! I know he loves me;
I'm sure his heart approves me;
My heart with joy is thrilling;
    An ecstasy divine,
My dreams of bliss fulfilling,
    For bliss untold is mine.

His love would never grieve me,
Nor e'er on earth deceive me;
He is an oak-tree lending
    Protection to the vine,
Whose leaves are interblending,
    Where climbing tendrils twine.

Forever will he love me,
None e'er be prized above me.
Around his heart I'm creeping,
    A close embrace is mine—
The branches overleaping
    As they to me incline.

Ah! may his love retain me,
His strength for e'er sustain me!
For I to him am clinging,
    A fragile, tender vine;
My leaves are swaying, swinging,
    But close my tendrils twine.

For climbing, may he love me;
For love, his heart approve me.
My heart its way is winging
   Where branch and tendrils twine,
And, nestling there, is singing
   Of joy and love divine!

EXALTED LOVE.

IN sensuous languor, complete—
We revel in reverie sweet—
An emotion enthralleth, and stills,
While the being with ecstasy thrills.

Oh, the grandeur of feeling, bestowing
That thrill—so transcendently glowing!
From the wonderful light of deep eyes,
Seeing heavenly transports arise.

Red lips are with eloquence dumb;
The mind to all reason is numb;
And yet all that mortal can feel,
Love's light in the eyes may reveal.

Indefinable magical spell,
Whose rapture no language can tell,
That proves, by the meeting of lips,
Love's pleasures all others eclipse.

Sipping nectar that never can cloy—
To swoon with a surfeit of joy—
We slip from the moorings of this,
And drift to the bright realm of bliss.

Oh, largess, supreme, infinite!
Sweet tremulous throb of delight!
All other conceptions above
Is the grand exaltation of love.

LOVE'S DREAM.

To limpid music, flowing rhyme,
  My heart keeps singing,
Like chiming-bells that all the time
  Joy-peals are ringing.

As waves of sound still rise and swell,
  Thus waves of feeling—
Emotions deep—with mystic spell
  Are o'er me stealing.

For beauteous thoughts through all my mind,
  Their way are winging;
Pure joy and bliss, with peace combined,
  These thoughts are bringing.

And every nerve in heart and brain
  Is throbbing, thrilling.
Ah, rapturous love, I wear thy chain,
  A captive willing.

Enwrapt in glowing dreams, I lie,
  So real the seeming,
'Twere e'en an ecstasy to die,
  So sweet the dreaming.

While sunburst gleams of Paradise
  Are round me falling,
Enshrined in bliss my spirit lies—
  Bliss most enthralling.

Hope and Memory.

HOPE AND MEMORY.*

I SEE a vision of enchanting guise,
　　More fair than royal Truth,
That looketh smilingly from out the eyes
　　Of guileless, happy youth.

'Tis Hope that lovingly walks, hand in hand,
　　With gladsome early Years—
Depicts the mirage o'er life's desert sand,
　　And shuns the vale of tears.

Bright Hope, that beameth in the child's sweet face,
　　So pure, so fair to see;
With joy endowing, and with artless grace
　　Of beauteous imagery.

Hope cheers the heart, and, each delightful day,
　　As guided oft by Truth—
To grand achievement, points the ready way,
　　Beguiling, beckons Youth.

Without thee, were not love, nor faith, nor creed,
　　And strangest rarity—
Without thy spirit to inspire the deed—
　　Of thoughtful Charity.

Thy magic veileth woe, the swift hours bring—
　　Discloses scenes sublime;
Dissolves the mount of care, and knows no king;
　　Save only ruthless Time.

---

* Hope and Memory are here typified by Hon. Horace P. Biddle, of Indiana, and Myla, the little daughter of the author.

Time's boon, dear Memory, lights the heart's demesne,
  'Tis Autumn's golden rod—
That with the sunset splendor, hue serene,
  Borders the path life trod.

Sweet Mem'ry, born of love, floods all the soul,
  And beams through mist of years,
As sunlight-gleam, so bright and beautiful,
  Shines through the rain-drop tears.

A winsome Sprite is Hope, that enters life
  With Youth's grand heritage;
The past doth Memory rule, through joy and strife,
  Philosopher and Sage.

I cling to Hope, who, whate'er ills betide,
  Dispelleth doubt and fear;
And Memory, faithful, shall with me abide,
  More glorious grow, and dear.

Both picture wondrous scenes, so quaint and rare,
  Entrancing while they last;
Hope gayly paints the future's realms all fair,
  While Memory limns the past.

Though Hope may falsely promise that my Art,
  Be writ on scroll of fame;
Yet, in some simple legend of the heart,
  Let Memory keep my name.

Without them, life were drear and void to me;
  Where'er on earth I roam,
May charming Hope and tender Memory
  Possess my heart, their home.

ELDEST, RICHEST, RAREST.*

AGE, 'tis true, improves the wine ;
   Time love's sweets can never cloy.
Richest vintage—ripe the wine—
   So pure love without alloy,
Precious gold is from the mine—
   Priceless, purest joy.

With love's wine the heart is blest—
   Eldest, richest, rarest—
I, with care and grief oppressed,
   Prize love e'er the dearest.
Near love's fountain let me rest—
   Love, the brightest, fairest.

Man may prune the tender vine,
   Its tendrils gain new strength ;
The heart so pruned by hand divine
   Bears perfect fruit at length,
For upward still its thoughts incline ;
   Thus trained, the heart gains strength.

Flowers of love take root in earth,
   And, though first leaves be riven,
To other tendrils putting forth
   Greater strength is given,
Upreaching e'er, though low the birth,
   Find perfect bloom in heaven.

---

* Written on receipt of a letter from a friend, inclosing some lines from Shelley's
unpublished poems.

DINNA FORGET.

SOME moments are far more precious than years
    When two hearts are thrilled with love's kiss,
And we soar, as earthward we cast our fears,
    To the Heaven of rapturous bliss.

The sweet confession my musa sings—
    May angels record it above—
That blissful moments a recompense brings
    When souls blend together in love.

"THE SPIRIT'S EMBRACE."

MY spirit greets you,
    Flies to, and meets you,
Like a birdling let loose, unfettered and free.
    And since it hath found you,
    It hovers around you,
As the bird round its nest in the sheltering tree.

    Its airy breathings,
    Like smoke-cloud wreathings,
May hold you in thrall as a bright phantasy.
    Does it whisper, "I love you,"
    Or sway you and move you?
Thoughts I may not utter it whispers for me.

    As leaflets are swaying
    When zephyrs are playing
O'er Æolian harp, waking sweet melody,
    Soul-whispers above you
    Are sighing. I love you,
Thus ecstasy's longing I'm breathing o'er thee.

Sweet visions of beauty,
Of love, and of duty,
Our spirits are taught by the spirit above;
As snow-flakes, which, meeting,
Their mission completing,
Dissolve, not in tears, but in essence of love.

Is it but seeming?
Am I but dreaming
Thy spirit and mine now are meeting in space?
The charm let us break not,
Dream on and awake not—
God blesses the union when spirits embrace.

I WILL NOT DOUBT.

You must not doubt me—thus say you;
Yet love oft blends with sweet distrust;
We doubt and love because we do,
And love and doubt because we must.

I will not doubt; no vague distrust
Shall chill the heart-throb warm for you,
For to be happy, still I must
Believe you, love—believe you true.

I will not doubt; nay, better far
That we on earth had never met,
Than that distrustful fancies mar
Love's joy, and bring a vain regret.

I will not doubt. Let others see
Thine imperfections all unite.
To all thy faults I blind will be,
Nor use my eyes for such a sight.

I will not doubt, while, to make white,
　All colors blended·one may see;
So all thy failings in my sight,
　United, shall perfection be.

I will not doubt—nor disbelieve
　Nor school my heart to love thee less;
For be thou fickle—I must grieve
　To lose thy loving tenderness.

I will not doubt—though joy be brief.
　My thought exultant flies to thee;
A doubt would change that joy to grief,
　So precious is thy love to me.

INCONSTANCY.

As footprint impressed on the sand,
　As shade that flits over the lea,
As bubble that bursts in the hand,
　So fickle thy loving shall be.

As zephyr that plays in the grove,
　As gem that is thrown in the sea,
So the constant ray of thy love
　Is engulfed by inconstancy.

As meteor flash through the dark
　Of midnight's empyrean blue;
As the glow of the sunbeam's spark
　That gleameth and fades with the dew.

As fickle as wind o'er the sea,
　As sweet as the breath of the grove,
As fair as the dew on the lea,
　And as fleeting, shall be thy love.

MY DARLING.

WHAT shall I say to my darling, my darling?
  What shall I bring to my love?
  What that a blessing shall prove?—
    A sunbeam of morning,
    A halo adorning
  The heart, I will bring to my love.

What shall I say to my darling, my darling?
  What shall I bring to my love?
    A rapture most sweet,
    A joy most complete,
    It is fitting and meet
  That, with love, I should bring to my love.

What shall I say to my darling, my darling?
  What shall I bring to my love?
    A heart full of feeling,
    Its love unconcealing,
    Its homage revealing—
  All these will I bring to my love.

I LOVE YOU.

I LOVE you, oh, darling! I love you.
  There's melody rising and filling
  My soul, with an ecstasy thrilling,
To the musical rhythm, I love you,
Oh, darling! my dear one, I love you.

I love you, oh, darling! I love you.
  Tumultuously throbs my emotion,
  As surges the billow of ocean,
Whose white-crested foam comes to love you,
Oh, darling! my dear one, I love you.

I love you, oh, darling! I love you.
  To love is a womanly glory.
  I love and my eyes tell the story.
In dreams my soul whispers I love you,
Oh, darling! my dear one, I love you.

I love you, oh, darling! I love you.
  Why longer attempt its concealing?
  My being is thrilled and revealing
To all the wide world that I love you,
Oh, darling! my dear one, I love you.

JUST BECAUSE.*

A WOMAN'S REASON.

I LOVE my love, but scarce know why
  I love my love so true.
The reason must be this, that I
  Do love—because I do.

Love has no reason, this we prove ;
  Then pray where is the use
To name a reason for my love?
  Love is love's own excuse.

---

* Published in sheet-music form by John Church & Co., Cincinnati.

Then ask me not the wherefore, pray,
  Love in my heart doth live;
That heart I give, and only say,
  I give—because I give.

The bird that builds its airy nest
  In leafy bough on high,
So round, so strong, so smoothly pressed,
  Knows not the reason why.

Love's like the bird that in the breast
  May build its home, I trow,
And hovers o'er its downy nest,
  Nor " wherefore" seeks to know.

Love is a priceless joy, I wist,
  And love is blind, they say,
Yet none his meshes may untwist,
  Nor break love's weave away.

Then put no price upon your love,
  Nor reason why 'tis true;
God's light doth shine in heaven above,
  Because—God bids it to.

Not for my beauty, that must fade,
  Though bright as noonday sun;
Nor for my wit, were I a maid,
  Would I be wooed or won.

Not for my grace nor worldly pelf,
  Nor fame nor treasure-trove;
But love me for my very self,
  And just because you love.

No jewels rare we prize above
  A love that's fond and true;
But if you love me, only love
  Me—just because you do.

A PALINODE.

TEACH me, teach me, how to love thee,
  Teach me how to win thy love;
Not the sun that shines above thee,
  Brighter than my joy, would prove.

Teach me, teach me how to love thee,
  Teach me how to tell my love;
Teach my thought to sway and move thee,
  Floating on the breath of love.

Teach me not—I know I love thee—
  Teach me not to tell, my love.
Now my spirit bends above thee,
  Sweet, receive my treasure-trove.

None there are I prize above thee,
  None whom I so dearly love.
If thou canst not say, " I love thee,"
  Oh, believe not that I love!

MY PET.

My beauty, my pet,
  Can I ever forget
That summer evening when first we met—
How my soul was entranced by your presence, my pet.

My dear little pet,
  I wish you would let
Me clasp you, and hold, and caress you, and yet,
My heart would keep throbbing and longing, my pet.

How can you, my pet,
    A heart idly fret,
When you have it secure in the snare you have set?
Oh, why be so cruel—why torture me, Pet?

    Oh, darling, my pet,
    You throw out your net
To allure, to ensnare me, and play the coquette;
A fair, heartless rosebud thou art then, my pet.

    My sweet one, my pet,
    My wee mignonette,
Thy spirit that lingers about me yet
Brings pleasure-thrilled pain and a longing for Pet.

    Oh, loved one, my pet,
    The first time we met
'Twas little I thought you would bring me regret
And a yearning desire to possess you, my pet.

THE SWEETEST LASSIE.

OF all the sweet lassies and all the dear cousins,
Though I love them so dearly and count them by dozens,
'Tis for her I most care, for none may compare
With my dear cousin Hattie, so gentle, so fair.

Her black eyes mean mischief; her hair hangs in curls,
And for making you happy she beats all the girls.
If her you should see, I'm sure that, like me,
In love with this bright peerless maiden you'd be.

Her voice is as clear as the clear rippling rill;
Her notes are as pure as the tones of a bell.
Like a siren she'll charm; may nothing e'er harm,
My bonnie bright Hattie down East on the farm!

I'd tell you how winsome she is, if I could—
How graceful and witty, and handsome and good;
And love her I do, and so, too, would you,
If only this bonnie sweet maiden you knew.

LOVE ME BEST.

My life is sad and lonely—
    An aching fills my breast—
Love's query haunts my being
    As wild bird haunts her nest,
Whose song in notes atremble
    Is, love me, love me best.

Thou may'st not love me only—
    Fair brows thy lips have pressed;
But, ah! I yearn to hear thee
    Say words that make me blest—
Thy voice to me the tend'rest,
    Whisper I love thee best.

I'm longing, grieved and lonely,
    Like child to be caressed;
To feel thy strong arm round me,
    To lean upon thy breast;
Through life beyond forever,
    To know thou lov'st me best.

A FANCY.

I WONDER if the silent night
Hath dreams for him, sweet dreams of me,
Where almost seems myself appears!
I wonder if at morning light

He sends the fleeting thought to me
My waiting spirit almost hears!
I wonder if such spell is wrought
That in his being he doth see
Emotions surge resistlessly!
I wonder if love strikes the key
Till hearts vibrate, with magic fraught,
And Nature's grandest minstrelsy,
The music of the spheres, is caught!
I wonder that a fairy thing
Like Love, that flits on wayward wing,
Should rule the heart and reign a king!

IS IT LOVE?

So "you cannot help but love me!"
   How can I believe?
Nay, I know not how to prove thee,
   Men will so deceive.

Thank you kindly, as you say so,
   For the love you bring,
Only fearing that love may so
   Very soon take wing.

Love is fickle as a shadow,
   Flitting here and there;
Over brook, or wood, or meadow.
   Flitting everywhere.

And you say I'm very sweet, sir ·
   How, sir, do you know?
And indeed it is not meet, sir.
   That you tell me so.

12

And you say that all the sweetness
  Of a hundred more,
Do but form the full completeness
  Of my honeyed store.

Ah, I fear you would deceive, sir.
  Feeding me with chaff;
Unbelievingly I grieve, sir,
  Doubtingly I laugh.

And you call me very good, sir;
  Hope I this is true;
I am very sure you should, sir,
  Try to be good, too.

And the feeling, rightly name it.
  Is it love, alone?
Let no baser passion claim it
  For its very own.

Love me truly, fondly, dearly,
  Let your love ne'er pall.
If you do not love sincerely,
  Love me not at all.

UNFETTERED.

As free as the air shall you be—
  As free as the zephyr at play
That flits o'er the meadowy lea—
  To tarry or wander away—
To love dearly, or not to love me.

Allegiance I would not compel,
   For love, like a bird in its flight,
May float over mountain or dell,
   Ere its pinions enfold to alight.
Where it choose, there it chooseth to dwell.

Nor constancy shalt thou declare,
   Nor seek to enslave love with art.
Like song-bird as free as the air,
   Love seeketh its haven, the heart—
Safely sheltered from harm nestles there.

So tenderly, broodingly low,
   It thrilleth the heart with its song,
As pure, and as clear, as the flow
   Of the brooklet that warbles along,
Illumined by sunbeam's bright glow.

As pure and as fair as the ray
   That gleams in the blue dome at e'en,
Ere cloudlets shall thitherward stray,
   And tempest shall gather between,
And fadeth the starlight away.

If flyeth thy love unto me,
   I'll tenderly cherish the guest,
Nor bind it to true constancy,
   Nor pledge nor environ it, lest
From bondage it hastens to flee.

MY OWN.

Most thrilling sound the lips have framed,
The dearest words that e'er were named,
Ah, truest truth the heart hath known,
Enclosed in simplest phrase, my own.

Enclosed, as in a waking dream,
In iridescent glow and gleam ;
Thus fancy's halo round me thrown
Thrilleth my heart with joy, my own.

The words, their form, their very sound,
I fold, with sweet thought wrapped around,
Close to the heart that now hath known
The rapturous bliss of love, my own.

A wind-swept harp in rhythmic strain
Expresses sweet ecstatic pain ;
So thrills my heart's deep undertone
To harmony of love, my own.

HE KISSED ME.

HE kissed me,
   And though 'twere against my will,
It stirred all my nerves
   With a strange sweet thrill ;
As bird o'er the brooklet
   That tippingly dips,
And toys with the wavelet
   It daintily sips.
Thus culled he the nectar
   That lurked in my lips ;
Until, so it seemed,
   While the sweets he quaffed,
That my heart came forth
   With the precious draught.
The memory of that loving kiss
Seems like a dream of a realm of bliss.
Softly it cometh and haunteth me,
Waking my being to ecstasy.

A STORM ON THE MATTERHORN.*

GRAY shades creep down from cliff to plain
  Into the deep ravine:
Lightning that rends the sky in twain
  With grandeur lights the scene.

A purple splendor looms between
  Blue depths, and amethyst;
Swift-marshalled, threatening clouds convene,
  And hide the curling mist.

The pines put on a mourning dress,
  Habiliment of woe—
And sob and moan in sad distress,
  As shadows darker grow.

The thunders roll, the hoarse winds roar,
  While lurid lightnings leap;
The storm bursts forth, its torrents pour
  Adown the rocky steep.

The angry storm-clouds, wrestling, wreath,—
  Rain-floods deep fissures plow;
And swirling winds rage far beneath,—
  The lofty mountain's brow.

Dark masses, meeting, swiftly shroud
  The mountain's base, yet see!
Far, far above the sombre cloud,
  The sun shines lovingly.

The giant peak with cap of snow
  Looming in cloudless height,
Sun-kissed, stands forth in gladsome glow,
  Unsullied, pure, and white.

---

* Suggested by a painting of the same by Albert Bierstadt.

The light reflects in amber tint,
   On summits lower down,
And touches with a golden glint,
   Their foliage green and brown.

And thus the clouds of sorrow o'er,
   And storms of human life,
The spirit may, triumphant, soar,
   Beyond turmoil and strife.

The soul serene, to sunlit skies,
   Above the mortal clod,
To Thought's high table-lands doth rise
   And bask in smile of God.

WITH GRACE OF TENDRILS TWINE.

FULL oft the tree and vine I've seen,
   With leaflets interlaced;
That, vine-wreathed tree, is like, I ween,
   The heart by love embraced.

They grow together strong and fair;
   Love's vine must die if rude winds part,
The tree looms up, despoiled, and bare—
   So like a loveless heart.

The heart survives, like tree, 'tis true,
   Of love bereft, like tree of vine;
Not as in beauty's strength it grew
   With grace of tendril's twine.

So we are like the tree and vine;
   A yearning love I own,
Whose clinging tendrils reach to twine
   'Round thy heart all bereft and lone.

A VIRELAY.

FOR his coming I've waited in vain,
  Waited and listened to hear
  The sound of his step drawing near,
Till the eve is beginning to wane.

I chide my sad heart, for I fain
  Would believe I have nothing to fear—
  No rival to him is more dear—
But my heart maketh doubting complain.

How long will he constant remain?
  A week, or a month, or a year,
  Till he findeth one more than my peer?
Will he turn from me then with disdain?

And what by the change will he gain?
  More beautiful she may appear;
  He will find not the love he found here—
The heart that ne'er gave him a pain.

O love, thou art bliss, or a bane,
  A whirlpool, a vortex most queer,
  And whoever life's vessel would steer
To thy realm must be surely insane.

LOVE MUST TEACH PHILOSOPHY.

I BRING thee on thy natal day
  Small tribute of a friend's regard;
Small profit it, the words I say,
  Since virtue brings its own reward.

Rejoice, though sorrow thou hast known,
   With trials, griefs, and joys and tears,
Since through these teachers thou dost own
   Wisdom and strength of fifty years.

Let rugged outlines disappear,
   Nor strive to show the stoic's art ;
Let every day and month and year
   More tender prove thy loving heart.

So, ripening in the perfect man,
   Thy life a lesson, too, shalt be,
And thou shalt find in God's great plan,
   That Love must teach Philosophy.

THE WITHERED MYRTLE (LOVE BETRAYED.)*

FRIEND, early on thy brow was a withered myrtle placed,
Closely "nettles" hedged thee in, for "scandal" thee embraced.
A monkshood's "poisonous words"—with these the air was rife,
And ruthless "nightshades" of "suspicion" hovered o'er thy life.
A "disappointed hope" the "cypress" brought, and also "dark
   despair."
E'en like bright flowers thy future looked, yet flowers may hide
   a snare—
A "pure white poppy's" ever fraught with either "good or ill ;"
And thee, ah, friend! 'twas doomed to heal, though healing it did
   kill.
Yet one more floral offering on thy memory's grave I lay,
While beside that grave most earnestly and fervently I pray

---

* An acrostic.—To find the name hidden in this acrostic, take the first letter of the
first line in connection with the second letter of the second line, the third letter of the
third line, and so on, when the name will thus appear—Flora K. Harding.

That all is with thee well.   Let these my offerings be,
First "Hawthorn Blossoms" only, yet they "hope invoke" for
    thee,
And a name wrought out in flowers with the thread of poesy.

THE ACME OF BLISS.

ART aweary and longing for rest?
  Let me soothe thee with lovingest art.
I will pillow thy head on my breast,
  Just over a warm, throbbing heart.

The lips that I love shall be pressed
  By the tenderest touch of a kiss,
Till thy being shall thrill and be blessed
  With fulness of rapturous bliss.

Shall I blushfully strive to conceal
  Emotions that mighty have grown?
'Twere in vain, for my eyes will reveal
  The sweet story—"I love you"—my own!

RHYMES TO LOVE.

MORE rhymes to love, the poet cries!
More rhymes to love, a swain replies,
In flowing rhythm, measured time,
To match with love some glowing rhyme.

Oh, poet soul or timid swain,
Thou hast no cause to thus complain;
List now to me, with lovers bold,
And I will tell how love is told.

For rhyme, or poet's flowery screed,
To picture love there is no need.
A wordless carol has the bird,
To sing of love without a word.

Love talks the language of the eyes;
The heart responds in dulcet sighs;
The blush that mantles Beauty's cheek
Doth oftentimes whole volumes speak.

An eye down cast, or tender glance,
Doth love's expression more enhance;
And none but lovers understand
How much is told in clasp of hand.

'Twere vain to number mystic signs
By which true love true love divines;
How tears and smiles the heart may move.
And all its deep affections prove.

The dearest thoughts, unsaid, unsung,
Tremble, unuttered, on the tongue;
Love's mead more sweet than wild-bee sips
Is nectar quaffed from dainty lips.

These tell the strength and tenderness
Which words are powerless to express;
Sigh speaks to sigh; its counterpart
Finds echo in an answering heart.

Let love be like the longing soul
That strives to reach the beautiful;
Pure and as deep as Heaven above.
Few rhymes may then suffice for Love.

JOYS OF AN ECSTASY PAST.

THE joys of an ecstasy past,
   The bliss of a loving caress,
While life in the bosom doth last,
   In the heart ever lingers to bless.

A mem'ry without a regret
   Proves real a midsummer's dream.
Blissful moments we never forget
   As we drift on time's hastening stream.

Nature's path leads up to the Lord;
   Her pleasures are free from alloy.
Nature's duties will bring their reward;
   Nature's book teach us how to enjoy.

LOVE'S PHILOSOPHY.

WHEN love reigns in the human heart
   Its thralls two souls enchain;
What strength can union's bondage part
   If constant, love remain?

Yet none love's fealty can see,
   Although it seem so plain,
Until by lover's constancy
   Time proves it doth remain.

We may discern the signal true—
   Know love-light cannot wane
When joy doth thrill the being through
   With ecstasy of pain.

A SIGH.

EACH fair beautiful day
Seems to mock us alway
When the heart is o'ershadowed with grief.
As the hours slowly fly,
Or the moments creep by,
In our sorrow we cry,
Oh, time, on thy wings bring relief!

Only sorrow and fears
They bring to us, the years,
Which we hoped would be laden with love;
And our heart, it appears,
Floats in deluge of tears,
Till hope's messenger-dove
The olive-leaf, Peace, finds above.

WERE MINE THE POWER.

WERE mine the power to bring, dear friend,
A birthday token meet for thee,
A host of joys should e'er attend
Thy every anniversary.

A wreath of hopes for thee I twine;
To thee may sorrows never come;
May richest love bless thee and thine,
The bud and bloom of thy dear home.

My simple words can scarce express,
Nor yet the loving thought impart
That thrills me with its tenderness,
And gives thee tribute from my heart.

ONLY A WOMAN.

No first-born son am I of titled peer,
  No daughter of a kingly line;
Inheritor of woman's hope, and fear—
  A woman's sole possessions, mine.

A woman's heart, wherein the fount of tears,
  Oft rising, overflows the eyes;
A woman's life, whereon the passing years
  Have writ their griefs and joys and sighs.

THE POET'S ERA.

TO O. F. A.

"THE world doth move; the earth is round;"
  Galileo's proof was plain;
The people scoffed. These words resound:
  "Oh, fool, thou art insane."

And thus in realms of science, art,
  Or philosophic lore,
Children of genius dwell apart—
  Their spirits lonely soar.

The poet limns with prescient art
  The world, humanity;
Though of the throng he seems a part,
  More clearly doth he see.

His heart with stricken ones of earth
  For human rights doth stir,
For fate decreed him at his birth
  A true philosopher.

He seems to dream; his spirit leaps
　　The future's dark abyss—
A hundred years the cleft, to reach
　　The era rightly his.

Incomprehensible, intense,
　　The poet-soul forlorn,
Is understood a century hence
　　By sages yet unborn.

RETRO ET PROSA.

THE delirium is over, the ecstasy past,
The sweet dream has vanished—'twas too sweet to last;
　　But the pleasure awakened by loving caress
　　Shall linger forever to comfort and bless,
For memory will treasure the bliss of the past.

Ah, joys that were brightest! Ah, dreams that have fled!
Ah, visions of lost love! Ah, hopes that are dead!
　　Will the future that waits for us over the main
　　Restore to our lives that lost Eden again?
Will our famishing souls with love's manna be fed?

INSPIRATION.

THE flood-gates lift, the torrents flow
　　In surging waves unending,
While in the skies with tinted glow
　　The sunset clouds are blending.

Through centuries the seasons roll,
  God's mighty power divining,
Till shall be reached the final goal
  Through Heaven's glory shining.

Emotions surging upward rise,
  In thrall my spirit holding,
While suns that shine o'er paradise
  Are bows of peace unfolding.

Emotions reach the realm of thought;
  My weary spirit, lifting,
Upon the wave of song is caught,
  That seems so idly drifting.

As Heaven's sunlight draws the rain
  From lifted waves to dower
The fevered earth, the thirsty plain,
  With sweet refreshing shower,

So onward, upward, fair and free
  The soul in song is flying;
As floating breath of ecstasy
  Is borne aloft in sighing

And every soul uplifted is,
  Some other spirit blessing,
And fructifies with chastened bliss
  Like dew-drop's fall, refreshing.

Through time and space majestic roll
  Diurnal orbs revolving,
Eternity is like the soul
  In ecstasy dissolving.

TO A PHYSICIAN.

WHAT skill shall cure that ceaseless ache
   Of heart with pain accurst?
Who can that quenchless longing slake
   For love, that yearning thirst?

I only ask surcease of pain;
   I seek not fame nor wealth.
A great physician thou, 'tis plain,
   Yet canst not heal thyself.

Then wherefore seek relief through thee
   For throbbing, quivering heart!
Thine own is aching, though thou be
   Well skilled in healing art.

LOVE LIVETH THROUGH DEATH.

I CLAIM not your fond adoration;
   No suppliant am I at your feet.
Free offering. self-abnegation,
   Is the love that is triumph complete.

I pledge you no symbol of honor,
   Yet queenly shall be the proud boast,
That the heart all unsought from the donor
   Is the gem to be valued the most.

We know that the briefest to-morrow
   A change to our being may bring—
May burden the heart with the sorrow
   That teaches the poet to sing.

Yet say when the death-dew is falling—
　In beads o'er my cold, pallid brow—
Shall your heart leap to mine in its calling?
　As tenderly answer as now?

Or then, shall your thought ever hover
　So near to my lone, narrow bed—
No longer adorer nor lover
　When my soul from its temple hath fled?

Exult, oh, my soul, in thy sadness,
　And heart whose death-knell hath been rung;
Love liveth through death, when in gladness
　Shall its song, now so voiceless, be sung.

———————

MYLA PETITE.

AH! how can I write of you, Myla petite?
　So bonny and sweet;
From the curl on your brow to your twinkling feet,
You are dainty and pretty, my love, my sweet.
　　Like the azury skies
　　Is the light of your eyes,
　Where the unspoken thought still heavenward flies
Like a bright winged bird, like yourself, my sweet.

And how can I sing of you, Myla petite?
　So bonny and sweet;
Whose lightest footfall I hasten to greet
And welcome the sound of your coming. my sweet.
　　Rhythmic lore, roundelays,
　　Cannot measure your praise
　Nor harmony compass your quaint, winning ways.
No melody thrills like your voice, my sweet.

Oh, what shall I say to you, Myla petite?
     So bonny and sweet;
How speak of the nameless charm so complete
That surrounds and envelops you, darling, my sweet?
     As the sun glints your hair,
     It would make you more fair,
     Were it not that you now are beyond all compare,
Oh, precious, my jewel, my pearl, my sweet.

I give you warm greeting, dear Myla petite,
     So bonny and sweet.
As, anon, midst the curious throng we meet,
And my heart rushes forth to you, Myla, my sweet,
     Will you crush out its beat
     With the tread of your feet?
     Then hasten away with your footstep fleet;
A tyrant thou art then, thou art, my sweet.

I long for your presence, dear Myla petite,
     So bonny and sweet.
My longing doth send me to fall at your feet;
You must know I love you, you know it, my sweet.
     Oh, my darling, confess
     That you love me, say yes
And seal the sweet promise with fondest caress;
Your love is my Eden, my life, my sweet.

MY HOME.

I HAVE sheltering nooks where none others abide,
     I have beautiful realms for my home,
Where in safety I dwell, where no evils betide,
     Where never disasters may come.
Wouldst know of this shelter whose roof-tree defends?
'Tis a home in the hearts of my friends.

SPIRIT BREATHINGS.

INSCRIBED TO T. B. A.

My spirit soars high, on the wings of thought,
   To the ideal realm of the mystic sphere;
Bright fancies, heavenward rising, are caught
   Like sun-rays that sparkle on burnished spear.

Though the weighted being mournfully lies,
   Enthralled by the carking cares of earth,
The spirit with rapture, untrammelled flies
   To the source of creation, whence came its birth.

Then rejoice with me that through realms afar
   My soul floateth free as a woodland bird.
My thoughts by the breath of the angelus are
   Vibrating with joy—are with ecstasy stirred.

Aye, rejoice with me that though chained to earth
   Remaineth the form, the spirit may rise
And soar to the heavenly realm of its birth
   To bask in the sunlight of paradise.

THE CULPRIT.

Guilty of loving? I fear it is true,
If to think is a crime, for I *think* I love you;
For I tremble with joy when I know you are near,
And your voice thrills my being throughout, my dear.

Thinkest thou not, like a simpleton, elf,
I am bringing the proof that convicts but myself?
Yet, "honor 'mong thieves," I the secret impart
To you as a thief, for you've stolen—my heart.

Love comes when he will, goes without being sent,
And I've surely committed no wrong *with intent;*
And I hope, as 'twas done without *malice prepense,*
You'll graciously pardon my loving offence.

PLATO'S DREAM.

TELL me not, when bright is glowing
   Pure and fair, love's holy flame,
When sweet thoughts in verse are flowing,
   Plato's dream was but a name.

As the current, stronger growing.
   Pours its fulness to the sea,
So shall love, beyond earth's knowing,
   Be life's current, still, to me.

Love shall be the seed I'm sowing,
   Whose fair buds shall bloom in rhyme,
Wealth of fragrant thought bestowing
   To futurity of time.

Hearts with purer thoughts imbuing,
   Love that Heaven will not blame—
Love the life of flowers renewing,
   Chapleting the brow of fame.

Love, albeit a love Platonic,
   Love devoid of every art,
Breathed in tender strains, euphonic,
   Finding echoes in the heart.

Throbs my heart with pure emotion;
   Free from passion it must be;
Love that flows to swell the ocean
   Of a broad humanity.

EDWIN BOOTH.

Her rays of golden light doth genius shed
Upon thy gifted brow. She o'er thy form
Her precious mantle casts, which thou, oh, Booth,
With mien majestic, royally dost wear.
And long time after thou hast left us for
"That undiscovered country, from whose bourne
No traveller returns," thy memory in
The minds of men, immortal shall remain;
For thou, thou art the child of genius true,
And genius is divine. In later years
When men shall seek by every specious art
The character to vividly portray
Of Hamlet, mad prince, yet counsellor wise
And most unfortunate in life's affairs,
They'll study thee—pattern thy leadership—
For those who would to Hamlet justice do
Must copy Booth. And thou immortal bard,
Whose teeming brain's creation Hamlet is,
Couldst thou but once return, revisiting
This mundane sphere, where art doth nature limn,
Thou'dst see thy Hamlet live again in Booth.

WYANDOTTE.

Memories, like tones, most sweetly ring.
And by their power a vision bring.
I see again that fairy grot,
Within thy caverns, Wyandotte.

Thus memory's echo lingers long,
Like sweet refrain of soulful song,
And then, oh, joy, 'tis my blessed lot
To see in dreams sweet Wyandotte.

And as the tones still rise and fall,
My heart responds to each and all;
In future years my mind shall not
Forget thy realms, oh, Wyandotte.

Oft as sweet memories swell and rise,
They bring the moisture to my eyes;
Thou'rt nature's child, without a blot
To mar thy beauty, Wyandotte.

At memory's touch my heart-strings thrill;
Were I the creature of my will—
I'd rest within an humble cot,
Beneath thy hill-side, Wyandotte.

With thoughts of thee my mind doth teem,
My fancies float as in a dream,
For on this earth there is no spot
So dear to me as Wyandotte.

Thou'rt nature's child, and nature's lyre
Kindles the soul's ecstatic fire,
And never canst thou be forgot,
God's fairest work, dear Wyandotte.

THE POET'S DREAM.

WHAT, then, is existence, and what is fame?
A dreamer's vision, an empty name.
And what the horizon that girds our sight?
A foothold to plume for loftier flight—
Through darkening clouds to glorious light.

The shadows are lifted—a passing gleam
Lighting the soul of the poet doth seem
To loosen the bonds that it upward may rise
To a restful shelter beyond the skies—
To revel in beauties of paradise.

A beautiful being from realms of thought
In the spirit of truth my soul hath sought,
And I welcome the presence within my breast
Of this angel of peace that promises rest—
The joys of heaven and home with the blest.

MY DARLING FOREVER.*

EVER, my darling, forever,
   Lean on the strength of my love,
Bound by sweet ties naught can sever,
   Joined by the spirit above.
Come to my arms and remember, love,
   They'll shelter thee e'er from the blast;
Storms of life's wintry December, love,
   Never thy sky shall o'ercast.

    Ever, oh, darling, forever,
      Precious one, dearest to me,
    Naught in this world can dissever
      Tendrils that bind me to thee;
    Naught in this world can dissever
      Love-links that bind me to thee.

So, though each coming to-morrow
   Bring thee of joy or of care—
Thine be a harvest of sorrow—
   Gladly thy troubles I'll share.
Listen! oh, heed my appealing, love!
   Be of my own self a part;
List while my lips are revealing, love,
   Longings that swell in my heart.

---

* Published in sheet-music form by John Church & Co., Cincinnati, Ohio.

Ever, oh, darling, forever,
  Precious one, dearest to me,
Naught in this world can dissever
  Tendrils that bind me to thee;
Naught in this world can dissever
  Love-links that bind me to thee.

I THINK OF THEE.

In peaceful noon of wistful night,
  When silence reigns o'er land and sea,
When beams the sky with silvery light,
  In watches lone, I think of thee.

When moves the sun, his radiant beams
  Forming a glorious pageantry
In path of Heaven, e'en then, in dreams,
  In waking dreams, I think of thee.

At dewy morn and starry eve
  Sweet, tender thoughts steal over me;
In Fancy's magic loom I weave
  Bright imagery, and think of thee.

A memory naught can e'er erase
  Sweeps o'er my soul and thrilleth me—
Brings to my mind thy thoughtful face—
  In dreams I see, I think of thee.

In dreams a strange mysterious spell
  Thy semblance limns. 'Twere plain to see
The why; I love thee, passing well,
  Therefore, dear one, I think of thee.

In dreams thou holdest me to thy breast,
  Our hearts accord in sympathy;
With love thy lips to mine are pressed,
  And thus, in dreams, I think of thee.

LOVE'S DECREE.

You say you have oft been *indited*,
  Which "indictment" I think may be true:
'Tis fitting, if I have the power,
  That I bring a "conviction" to you.

This writing, the silent "witness,"
  Will the proof of your guilt impart;
This *inditement* convicts you a felon,
  And proves you have stolen—a heart.

And so you are "found" by the *jury;*
  Step forward and learn my decree:
You must yield up the heart you have stolen,
  Or your own, in return, bring to me.

WILT THOU BE MINE?

He sang to me in sweetest strain
Of melody, with low refrain;
And tenderly upon my soul,
The music swept all beautiful.
Refrain.—Wilt thou be mine, he sang to me,
        My own, my own, fore'er to be?
        Some day, dear heart, tell me some time
        Thou wilt be mine, thou wilt be mine.

Hast thou a heart to give, sang he—
A little love to spare for me?
Then soft and low the music grew—
I love you true, I love you true.
Refrain.

My soul responded to the call,
While love my senses held in thrall;
And yet, the words I could not say,
I will be thine, some day, some day.
Refrain.

That pleading air affects me still;
The words yet make my bosom thrill:
And wake my heart to love's distress,
To sympathy, and tenderness.
Refrain.

Oh, tender heart, oh, friend sincere.
Oh, loyal soul, I hold so dear,
Would I might echo back the strain,
And join thee in the sweet refrain.
Refrain.

    Wilt thou be mine, he sang to me,
    My own, my own fore'er to be?
    Some day, dear heart, tell me, some time
    Thou wilt be mine, thou wilt be mine.

TO JOAQUIN MILLER.

WITH infinite joy I am greeting
  Thy beautiful thoughts, dear friend;
Emotions in sympathy meeting
  Are lofty as snow-mountain's trend.

I have coined tender thoughts as a token
  From a heart that is true to the core;
Little need, that in words they be spoken—
  The mind hath its own mystic lore.

So clearly the spirit divineth
  The feeling no language hath told,
And tenderly, lovingly shrineth
  The fealty stronger than gold.

Oh, brother, and poet most loyal
  In all that these titles portend,
There is nought under Heaven more royal
  Than the unselfish love of a friend.

As steady as flight of the eagle—
  As true as the needle to pole—
As fair and as pure and as regal
  As an untarnished beautiful soul—

Yet humanly tender, ne'er grieve it,
  For faith, love, and charity blend
In the link that uniteth; receive it,
  The hand-clasp that pledges thee, friend.

THE TRYST.

I LINGERED and listened, with longing, to hear
The sign of his coming, a step drawing near;
And I lovingly deemed, and still hope it may be,
When my thought flies to him, that his thought seeketh me.

I shunned the gay circles and hastened to-night
To welcome his coming with glow of delight;
To see in the fathomless depth of his eyes
The eloquent feelings tumultuously rise.

To thrill with emotion and inwardly feel
The joy of devotion, a look may reveal;
For the depth and the measure of love's tenderness
Our language hath never the word to express.

BIRTHDAY WISHES.

I WISH, on this auspicious day,
All that may bring thee peace and joy;
That sunshine beam upon thy path;
That fortune yield the store she hath;
That sin ne'er lead thy steps astray;
Thy pleasure be without alloy.

All these I wish, and wishing still,
Would pray thee make more high thine aim.
Let nought a noble purpose blight
That should attain the loftiest height.
May future years these hopes fulfil,
And add bright lustre to thy name.

CLOUDS OF LIFE AND SKY.

HIDING the light, dim shadows lie;
These, at approach of others, fly;
Great hills of vapor intervene
To hide the moonlight's silvery sheen.

Winged shadows flit athwart the sky;
So clouds between my life and I
Gather and flit, or linger yet,
Faint shadows of a vague regret.

Midsummer clouds o'er sunset sky,
Like changing years, go swiftly by ;
Or reuniting, darkly roll ;
Thus storms of grief sweep o'er the soul.

The lightest clouds that fleck the sky
May grow still lighter by and by ;
If, gathering fast, they bring the rain,
The sun will surely shine again.

Through rifted rocks the light descry
The star that guides our hopes on high.
The darkest night must pass away,
And after dawn comes perfect day.

When darkest cloudage dims life's sky,
Look far beyond with faith's clear eye.
The storm will make the air more pure,
Life's sorrows teach us to endure.

MY MOTHER DEAR.

DEAR beaming eyes, dear saintly face
That picture forth a spirit's grace,
Though criss-cross lines old time hath wrought,
Here sits enthroned the noblest thought.

Thy mother-love its joys impart
From sunny realms within thy heart :
Far-reaching in its tenderness,
Surrounding cherished ones to bless.

Dear earnest one, thy precepts mild
Have wrought their mission through thy child ;
Made her life work a ministry
Whose inspiration comes through thee.

Thy purified and lovely soul,
Through sorrow grown more beautiful,
Still seems to hover near the skies,
And point the way to Paradise.

THE WEDDING BELL.

Peal forth, oh, merry wedding bell,
For Isabelle, for Isabelle;
And as the silvery tones ascend,
In gleeful rapture may they blend
The voiceless sounds "do well, do well."
Aye, joyous echoes rise and swell
For Isabelle, fair Isabelle;
A wealth of happiness foretell,
Oh, marriage bell, for Isabelle.
My thought keeps time, keeps throbbing time,
Like tinkling bells, to music's chime,
And sends a peal, (appeal) in rhyme,
Her gladsome future thus to tell;
For how can bonnie Isabelle
Do other than do well, "do well?"

ALL AWAKEN TO LOVE.

There are beautiful thoughts, low-buried,
And as beautiful songs unsung,
As have thrilled the heart of a nation
Or flowed o'er the eloquent tongue.

There are visions most real in seeming,
Emotions our being that move;
There are fancies that brighten our dreaming—
All awaken in answer to love.

IF LIFE MEANT ONLY LEISURE.

If life meant only leisure,
  Like childhood's hour of play;
We'd revel then in pleasure,
  While love our hearts should sway,
  And rapture crown each day.

Aye, love should be the treasure
  That in our hearts should stay,
While bliss in rhythmic measure
  Should sing love's roundelay,
  And joy should reign alway.

A CHARMING MYSTERY.

SURELY I was only dreaming,
  When it seemed her eye met mine,
And appeared as though 'twere beaming
  With a rapture half divine.
    For I found her a surprising,
    A tormenting, tantalizing,
    Very charming mystery.

Sendeth she my nerves a dancing
  Like the sparkles on the wine,
And my thought flies forth, romancing
  As a votary, at her shrine.
    But she is a quaint, surprising,
    A tormenting, tantalizing,
    Very charming mystery.

Oftentimes I'm sure I know her,
Read her thoughts, as I opine,
And I long for speech, to show her,
Feelings, words can scarce define.
But I find her a surprising,
A tormenting, tantalizing,
Very charming mystery.

Seemeth now, if I should meet her,
That my arms would round her twine ;
Longing, lovingly to greet her,
If she gave assenting sign.
But she is the most surprising,
Most tormenting, tantalizing,
Most bewitching mystery.

I COME TO LOVE THEE.

I COME in spirit, and I hover near thee ;
Thy longing for a presence still to cheer thee,
Doth henceforth evermore to me endear thee—
I come to love thee.

And ere I come and lowly bow before thee
Thou seest, love, and knowest I adore thee,
E'en when afar, in spirit bending o'er thee,
I come to love thee.

Thus loving, I love dearly to caress thee,
Close to my throbbing heart I love to press thee,
To breathe sweet incense o'er thee that may bless thee—
I come to love thee.

What though thy languid blood is fast congealing ?
Thy heart shall wake to richer, warmer feeling,
For I come warmest, deepest love revealing ;
I come to love thee.

Thy spirit through thy verse breathed forth a longing,
That claimed myself as to itself belonging,
And thus commingling loving thoughts came thronging ;
     I come to love thee.

Thy thoughtful wisdom makes me more revere thee ;
Thy kindly goodness doth the more endear thee ;
Thy love doth make it Eden to be near thee ;
     I come to love thee.

TO H. R. A.

ANOTHER year goes quickly past—
Time's wingèd mile-posts fly so fast ;
And here and there another thread
Of silver tint, adorns thy head.

What matters if the coming year
Brings added lines which prove how near
Old age approacheth ? Duty done,
E'en lines of care are laurels won.

By work and growth, in God's great plan,
Is perfected the noble man ;
By work and growth comes happiness
And strength, through life, to onward press.

Man's mind, like time, brooks no delay,
But marches forth to win the day ;
And time shall bring thee recompense
In Heaven's grand inheritance.

OII. LUSTROUS DEPTH.

OH, lustrous depth of wistful eyes,
    Whose glow illumes thy pensive face,
Whose splendor bids my thoughts arise
    To picture forth a spirit's grace.

For chiefest of thy charms to me
    Is that, withal thy queenliness,
In this fair semblance, plain I see
    Thy power divine, to cheer and bless.

God made thee fair and beautiful;
    He made thy lot more bright than mine.
God gave us both a longing soul,
    And wistfully my thought seeks thine.

My thought would hold commune with thine
    The while I view thy counterpart;
For surely, in so pure a shrine,
    God must have placed a loving heart.

NO CROSS NO CROWN.

THIS holy Easter morn
A glorious hope doth seem to enfranchise
My pinioned thought, and bid it upward rise
And soar away to realms beyond the skies;
    For Christ redeemed, new born,
In spirit riseth now to dwell in Paradise.

Oh, lustrous depth of wistful eyes,
Whose glow illumes thy pensive face.

On earth, a cross he bore—
Unmurmuringly he bowed beneath the load ;
Tyrants, inhuman, still beside him strode,
To drive him on, with taunt and sneer and goad ;
　　His anguished heart was sore—
Along his pathway tears of blood fast flowed.

　　So may a crown be won—
To bear a cross through all life's weary way ;
To humbly bow, yet upward strive, and pray
For strength to bear the burden day by day,
　　"Father, thy will be done,"
Learning with steadfast, childlike faith, to say.

　　Though all the world should frown
And gibe and sneer, and hold me up to scorn,
As one to spirit-meek, yet newly born,
I, too, shall rise, like Christ on Easter morn,
　　And wear a glorious crown,
Of fadeless flowers without a single thorn.

NEARER TO GOD.

I CLIMB to the height where it seemeth
　　That human foot scarcely hath trod ;
And ardently, fancy now dreameth,
　　That I am the nearer to God.

The branches uplifted are swaying,
　　Of tall trees that bendingly nod,
As they to the lowly were saying,
　　We also are nearer to God.

My spirit on airiest pinions
　　Above the sublunary clod,
Uprising to Thought's fair dominions,
　　Comes nearer, yea, nearest to God.

TO ME SHE IS NOT DEAD.

To me she is not dead,
Although where'er my wand'ring feet may tread,
In old familiar walks or distant spot,
   I seek, but find her not.

   And yet, in dreams I see
At midnight hour her form bend over me.
Her voice, as all through life, again I hear
   Breathe helpful words, sincere.

   Oh, Annie, where art thou?
With tender smile art hovering near me now—
Oh, sunbeam smile, dispelling cloud of care—
   About my study-chair?

   Ye, who have missed a friend,
Who vanished ere was reached your journey's end.
Ye also look in vain for dear face, fair,
   Nor find it anywhere.

   I know the Master said
" She only sleepeth," nay, she is not dead,
In garment of invisibility
   She yet abides with me.

   Oh, Sister of my Soul,
Dear, earnest spirit, true and beautiful,
I feel thee near; shall see thee, too, some day,
   When shadows pass away.

THE BADGE I WEAR.

TO H. M. B.

LONG time a heavy cross I bore—
   As fitting, lo,
Its pearly counterpart I wore,
   The badge of woe.
To calm my soul, by sorrow tried,
   Hope whispered low;
And bade me lay the cross aside—
   'Twere better so.

An anchor, then, the badge of Hope—
   Blessing sincere—
Replaced the cross, inspiring zeal to cope
   With grief and fear.
Meanwhile the simple, pearly pin,
   Grew, year by year,
Like laurel wreath that heroes win,
   More prized and dear.

'Twas stolen then, or on the ground
   Fell, here or there;
I searched unceasingly, nor found
   It anywhere.
A white pearl anchor now, I see,
   On breast more fair;
And henceforth envy dwells with me,
   Her badge I'll wear.

THE CIVIL ENGINEER.

INSCRIBED TO CAPTAIN J. B. EADS.

WHAT wondrous resource hath the human mind,
  How vast the cultured skill,
With force the warring elements to bind,
  Controlling them at will!

Driving the engine up the mountain-side,
  Panting like sentient thing;
It spans the fissured canyons deep and wide,
  And to the steep doth cling.

To bring immensity to smallest place,
  To bind the lightning's glare;
To circumnavigate terrestrial space,
  The ocean, and the air.

To bridge the current swift; 'neath swirling tide,
  To plant the solid pier;
To join great oceans, mountain-lands divide,
  Bring all the world anear.

To tunnel through the flint-like towering steep,
  Darker than tiger's lair;
To drill and blast the rocks beneath the deep—
  Place safety's signal there.

Aye, wondrous resource hath the human will,
  A strength devoid of fear.
Mighty the science, unexcelled the skill,
  Of Civil Engineer.

CHRISTMAS DREAMS.

Night before Christmas, you bear on your wing,
   Fancies so bright and hopes full of joy ;
Like chiming carols, they merrily ring
   From cherry-red lips of each girl and boy,
"I wonder what 'Santa' will bring ?"

Beautiful eyes now are hidden from sight,
   'Neath fringed white lids that over them close ;
Sunny curls fall with a softening light
   Shading the pillow where sweetly repose
Our little ones lovely and bright.

Love's sweetest lispers now dreamingly, sleep ;
   They watched for "Santa" long as they could,
At length, so sleepy, to bed they creep,
   While baby said, "Tell him bring somsing dood."
Bright angels, your watch o'er them keep.

Sleeping, their visions of dolly or drum,
   Like vapors, are floating airily by ;
Soldiers and trumpets and sweet sugar-plum
   In seeming, all night rise before them or fly,
Fairy fancies that go and come.

Visions of childhood, so joyous and sweet,
   Happiest hours when life is new ;
As Christmas dawns you so hopefully greet,
   E'er may your brightest of dreams come true,
Your gladness, your bliss to complete !

Beautiful eyes, may you waken to joy,
   As the Christ-child blesses each humble home !
To household darling, or motherless boy,
   May Santa Claus never forget to come,
Bringing pleasure without alloy !

DARE TO DO RIGHT.

TO MY SON.

DARE to do right! to be gentle, yet strong,
As on life's highway you journey along.
Ever be helpful and hopeful and true,
So shall a blessing be meted to you.

Dare to do right! for thy mother's sake, boy.
Thrilling her bosom with holiest joy:
Dare to be merciful, never afraid;
Lend to the helpless and needy thine aid.

Dare to do right! dare to always be brave;
From danger and sorrow seek others to save;
Shun ever the wine-cup, dare to say no:
In paths that you traverse another may go.

Dare to do right! dare to gladly say yes;
Such a reply may some weary heart bless.
Bravely press on till thy journey is done:
With courage and zeal are life's battles won.

Dare to do right! make thy course, like the lark,
Onward and upward and true to the mark.
With bright beacon-lights may Faith, Hope, and Love
Pilot thee safely to Heaven above.

TO LAWRENCE BARRETT.

GENIUS, by royal countersign,
Gives thee to enter realms divine;
Thy mind a talent loaned, a trust,
Thou hast not idle left, to rust.

'Tis long, full long, aye, many a day
Since erst I saw thee, "Elliot Grey."
Each hour that deep has scrolled thy name,
More clearly blazons forth thy fame.

What matter, though the passing year
Hath brought a joy, perchance a tear,
Or line of thought, thy part well done,
E'en lines of care are laurels won.

But I may not thy homage sing,
My rhymes but simple tributes bring;
To wish thee joy, to honor thee
For working out thy destiny.

As years shall make their ceaseless round,
May loftier notes thy praises sound,
Till Time, on topmost list of fame,
In golden letters, writes thy name.

TO A. B.

Art thou, indeed, a (vagrant) bee
Culling the sweets from every flower,
'Midst amaranthine bloom dost rove,
And nectar sip of woman's love,
An arrant thief, yet fair to see?

To realms of thought, in ecstasy,
I soar beyond your wanton power.
I roam with fancy far above,
To revel in ideal love
And cull the sweets of poesy.

But no! thou art a (working) bee,
Art hiving sweets each precious hour;
Rare wealth of thought, dear wealth of love,
My humble songs so far above;
That I, a drone, must seem to be.

DOUBT NOT.

'Tis he of little faith
　Who, when the sunshine glows
And flowers adorn his path,
　With fickle thought a doubt bestows
For all the good he hath.

How painful, yet how sweet
　Is love and doubt and joy!
The rose is incomplete
　Without its thorn; without alloy
No bliss on earth we meet.

Yet woman's trusting love
　Is true, and sweet, and sure,
Nestling like Heaven's own dove,
　As fair and as divinely pure,
Descending from above.

Richest who giveth most,
　Asking for no return;
Aye, this shall be love's boast,
　Who loveth most its truth may learn,
Truth proved by loving host.

Perchance a pleased surprise,
　Though I may not behold,
Beameth within your eyes,
　Seemeth, as I my thoughts unfold,
I, too, before you rise.

Love's ties are those that bind,
　For love will claim his own,
Though love unwisely blind,
　With sorrow must for bliss atone,
Yet keeps his idol shrined.

Never with doubt nor fear
  Distrust a love so fair,
Breathing its message dear,
  "Oh, darling! I would I were there!"
Or, "Would, love, you were here!"

MY OWN, MY DEAR ONE.*

(A SERENADE.)

My love, my life, my own, my dear one,
  My precious near one,
  My sweet sincere one;
How void is life without thy blessing,
  Thy fond caressing,
  Thy love expressing;
So dark, so void, so vain.

Oh, say, my own, you e'er will love me,
  Fore'er approve me;
  None prize above me;
So shall we have the sweet delight, love,
  The rapture bright, love,
  Joy's radiant light, love;
While life and love remain.

So shall two hearts light as a feather,
  Be joined together,
  With silken tether;
Each heart athrill with blissful feeling,
  Love unconcealing,
  Love's joy revealing;
Life hath no more to gain.

---

* Published in sheet-music form by John Ellis & Co., Washington, D. C.

NOBODY, NOBODY KNOWS.

AND who is it, then, that inspires my pen?
  Nobody, nobody knows.
It might be brother, or cousin; but then,
  It is—none of those.

Who is it that claimeth my waking thought?
  Nobody, nobody knows.
Brothers or cousins—perhaps now it ought
  To be some of those.

Who is it that visits me in a dream?
  Nobody, nobody knows;
It ought, perhaps, but it never does seem
  Like any of those.

Who is it loves me above all the rest?
  Somebody, somebody knows.
Brothers nor cousins could make me so blest;
  It is none of those.

Why does he love me? Can any one tell?
  Nobody, nobody knows.
Why do I love him, you question? Ah! well—
  He is not like those.

So shall we go loving on to the end?
  Nobody, nobody knows.
Brother nor cousin is he, but a friend
  Far dearer than those.

HE TOLD ME SO.*

A DEAR little maiden, bonny, bright maiden,
   Sweet little maid I know.
Her cheeks are like roses, lips are twin cherries,
   Her eyes are with mischief aglow.
And oft she is singing, glad as a bird,
   As glad as a song-bird is she.
She is so sweet, so true, discreet,
So fair, so neat, so quaint, petite,
   And this is the reason why :—

Refrain.—Somebody met her on the way,
      Walking adown the glen one day,
      Telling a secret, whispering low
      Love me, oh, darling, I love you so!
      Somebody's laugh is full of glee,
      Somebody loves me, carols she ;
      Somebody loves me dearly, I know,
      Somebody does, for he told me so.

Said he, Prithee, give me this hand, dear maiden,
   And with it thy love so true.
Her heart, then, she missed it, and found he possessed it.
   So what could the dear girl do,
But gayly go singing glad as a bird,
   For glad as a song-bird is she.
So fond, so dear, he did revere
The maid sincere without a peer,
   And this is the reason why :—

Refrain.

---

* Published in sheet-music form by Ellis & Co., Washington, D. C.

AT THE FARM.

INSCRIBED TO OLIVER WENDELL HOLMES.

On a rainy autumn morn
I, like pilgrim, wet and worn,
    Sought his door:
While anticipation sweet,
Like the wind down Beacon street,
    Flew before.

Thus upon the steps I stood
In that "attic" neighborhood
    Of the "Charles."
Oh, the tears—umbrella shed—
Oh, the veil, about my head
    Blown in snarls!

Waited I, in reeking trim,
Till a visage grave and grim
    Did appear.
"Dr. Holmes I called to see"—
Then the grave one answered, "He
    Is not here.

"He is growing old, you see,
And it suits him best to be
    At the farm."
Of "poor" farms I know, thought I,
Where poor people go, to die
    Far from harm.

But how rich that place must be,
That, for such an one as he,
    Hath a charm!
Selfish mortals all are we,
And I envied Beverly—
    That's the farm.

WAR POEMS.

THE GRAND ARMY OF THE REPUBLIC.*

IN years agone, a fearful strife was ended,
And hosts of valiant men who came together
At their country's call, summoned to combat,
Whose name was legion when they started forth,—
Were now dispersed; o'er this broad land
From east to western shores were widely scattered,
And resumed their peaceful avocations
In field or shop, as ere they went to war.
The clanking swords and sabres in quiet
Graced the wall, with gleaming bayonets sheathed;

---

* A sketch of the inception and growth of the G. A. R., written at the request of the
Executive Committee for the National Encampment at Baltimore, June 21, 1882, and
dedicated to the Grand Army of the Republic.

The muskets now in dusky corners stacked,
Rested, and rusty grew, while, bent to duty,
The patient shoulders, where they had been borne,
Were placed to move the wheels of industry
Which once more sang, with an unceasing hum,
The song of peaceful labor, honest toil.
But, o'er the land, so late baptized in blood,
Was tender grief mingled with loyal joy
In quiv'ring depths profound of aching hearts.
Oh, sad, sad hearts, which yet can scarcely say
" Thy will be done"—can scarcely feel a joy,
Which comes through grief—what touch of sympathy
Can reach thy hidden well-springs, heal thy woe ?
So sacredly doth memory treasure sorrow,
Art cannot hide the scenes her tablets bear.

Our spheres in life are narrow, hearts but human.
And it seems another generation
Must pass away, ere sorrow finds its tomb,
So long it lives, so lingers with us, though
By thrill of lofty patriotism subdued.
Oh, mothers, widows, daughters, sore bereft !
Would words of mine could move the government
To make its wards, these sorely stricken ones,
Suffering, not grief and sorrow only—
Nay, joined to illness, oft destitution
Adds grievous burdens to the wounded hearts
Whose loved ones fought for noble principles.
Aye, these should be our country's sacred charge.
Nations make haste to action tardily ;
The wheels of human progress move but slow,
Yet time shall surely bring a just reward.
Here or hereafter " time sets all things even."
Sustained by earnest loyal hearts,
Now and hereafter, this great government,
Whose banners float upon the dalliant breeze,
Planted by willing hands in Southern soil,
Shall yet do greater justice to the men

Who marched as its defenders, wore the blue,
Preserved that standard, kept its stars undimmed,
Till one united people shelter found
'Neath its broad folds; while now, oh, thrilling sight!
Victor and vanquished meet with clasping hands,
It stirs, at every motion waves a welcome.

As erst my muse declared was warfare ended,
And e'en a twelvemonth, too, had passed away,
Since grand review, and final muster-out,
When a strange germ in memory's garden grew.
For months this tender thought had lain, deep hid,
Like a spring flower that sleeps 'neath wintry snows,
Till balmy seasons call its tendrils forth.
Thus mem'ry touched the germ in many hearts,
And woke Fraternal Feeling in the breasts
Of comrades who had shared the weary march;
From same canteen had quaffed the cooling drink,
Assuaging thirst intense of famished men,
Who, shoulder to shoulder, had met the foe;
Where fiercest carnage raged had borne the brunt,
And had together faced its scenes of horror.
Then midst the loyal lads o'er all the States,
In field and shop, and busy mart wide severed,
The feeling grew, a yearning unsuppressed,
To see and greet again those fellow-soldiers.
This longing found expression and response;
Some met, were thrilled with joy, and organized
This loyal, true, and mighty brotherhood,—
Grand Army of the Republic.

                    Thus was formed
The nucleus small, of numbers few,
Round which now stand two hundred thousand comrades.
Was Loyalty its test and basis firm,
And with Fraternity, presided there.
These two were wed, and from this union true
Came Charity, which is greater than all.

15

These soldiers' hearts are swayed by unseen motors.
They are united by a wondrous tie,
A mystic link inured by battles dared,
Strong joined, aye, welded too, by dangers shared.
The tenderest, strongest bond known to the heart
Art thou, Fraternity, thy strength and power
Doth draw thy votaries from homes remote.
Thy greeting warm, like grand and stirring anthems,
Makes their pulses throb with more than brothers' love.
By camp-fires lighted in a thousand towns
Do comrades bring the wealth of memory's store;
The symbols keep of war's vicissitudes;
Join hands in holy realm of sympathy;
And annually the Grand Encampment meets,
And year by year grows large with added numbers.

A glorious scene! on Southern soil convened
Where Baltimore, fair city, welcome gives.
A score of years gone by, the greeting differed.
That scene is past, thank Heaven! forever past;
And ye can say to this fair citadel,
"Our fathers, too, were of its brave defenders."
Here stand once more those turbaned, fierce Zouaves,
Whose perfect drill, and bayonet charge, rouse wonder,
Yet cause no stir of fear; and stranger sight,
Behold, here gathered are the former foes
Who wore the gray, welcoming now, with cheers.
What meaneth this? Rejoice, the strife is ended.
They fought for what they deemed was right,
None the less bravely perilled life, and lost;
This Army Grand is armed but with forgiveness.

For months have willing hands made preparation,
Fraternal hearts, planned a joyous meeting,
And soldiers gather from the coast of Maine,
And from the borders of the chain of lakes.
They come from California's golden shore.
From Middle, Western, and from Southern States

They haste, to yet renew this tie that binds
Them all as brothers.   Titles are but sounds ;
One good name, Comrade, outranks all the rest.

Herein doth Charity in lovely guise
Bring to its cause a band of women true.
Like min'stering angels they, as years pass by,
Lend their support, and with their helpful hands
Aid to perpetuate its principles;
To smooth the war-scarred soldier's path through life;
To soothe the widows, help the brotherless,
And rear and educate the comrade's orphan;
For in a woman's heart lives patriotism,
Lofty as man's, as true, as daring.

Now silent messages are wafted here,
Where meets again the annual convocation,
From absent comrades, by thought's swift exchange;
And one can almost hear unspoken words
Of brothers far from hence; feel their warm grasp,
Know that invisible throngs their presence bring.

So shall this order prosper, lifted o'er
All party wrangle or dissentious strife,
And gather hosts of veteran recruits,
Till ten years pass—fast fall the soldiers old—
And then, shall surely come the less'ning ranks,
With no more volunteers from whom to choose.
Then one by one shall all be mustered out,
Yet, answer to a glorious reveille,
And join the comrades who have gone before—
In Heaven shall gather in an army grand,
To form one universal brotherhood.

ꝟ ARLINGTON.

WE leave the rolling heights of Arlington
As in the west the clouds, low hung,
Wear golden, radiant gleams, forth flung
  In slanting spears of light,
    Which evening sun
Delights to cast, afar and wide,
In shimmering waves of shade to hide
  Their sunny depth from sight.

Old home of Lee, o'erlooking Washington!
In silence rise those ancient halls
Where, erstwhile, startling bugle-calls
  Woke echoes in resound.
    Now battle's done.
The quaint old house a relic stands
Of scenes gone by, where spectre bands,
  Shades of the past, are found.

Thou stand'st deserted, lit by sinking sun.
Like gate through which old feuds have fled,
Resounds no more, to heavy martial tread,
  Thy well-worn oaken floor,
    Nor booming gun.
The cannon's deep-mouthed voice is dumb,
Is heard no more the roll of drum.
  Death wins; the conflict's o'er.

For now thy height, oh, peaceful Arlington!
Where roar of cannon did resound,
Is peopled thick, built up with many a mound;
  And silence, deep and dread,
    Through death is won.
A nation's dead fill soldiers' graves;
Above, our country's standard waves
  O'er city of the dead.

O'er mounds where heroes sleep at Arlington
Our thoughts keep guard with noiseless tread
Round silent bivouac of the dead ;
   Prayers, wafted to the skies,
    For every one,
Who, fearless, war's dread perils braved ;
Who with their lives the Union saved—
   With floral incense rise.

Long may'st thou stand, old house at Arlington !
When loftier structures pass away,
May still thy walls loom upward aged and gray,
   Guarding death's city well ;
    Like veteran son
Keeping a faithful watch and ward
O'er all who sleep beneath thy sward,
   Thou voiceless sentinel.

THE VETERAN CORPS.

BUT a handful of men is the Veteran Corps.
Whose roster is numbered in only threescore ;
But when clouds of rebellion did threatening lower,
Duty's laurels they won 'midst the cannon's dread roar.

For these veteran heroes, who muskets bore,
Represent each division or army corps,
And in honoring them, we do honor to all
Who answered the summons—our country's first call.

They were beardless boys when they started forth,
These true soldier lads of the loyal North ;
In the rank and file they have proven their worth,
Though many were wounded, and fell to earth.

At Antietam were some, and there may be one
At that first famous fight at Bull Run who did run.
Nor have I a doubt, could we name him, he'd tell
How when running, as fighting, he did it well.

When discretion was valor he ran away,
Thus he lived to do battle another day.
At Fredericksburg when the havoc was rife,
With Burnside were some in the thick of the strife.

And at Chancellorsville some of these had a share
Of fighting and danger confronting them there.
Here is one who remembers the bloody field
At Shiloh where foemen were ready to yield.

At the Gettysburg battle were two or three
Of these men who took part in defeating Lee;
Under Sickles and Hancock and General Meade,
With losses of Reynolds, Zook, Farnsworth, and Weed.

Disastrous the warfare, two days it was waged,
And carnage of battle incessantly raged.
Here comrades by thousands were slaughtered each day,
Or, dying and wounded, were carried away.

Of the Cumberland Army, here's one can tell
Of that scourging fire like the flames of hell,
When at Chickamauga they suffered defeat,
And the Union troops were obliged to retreat.

And another, of Spottsylvania's fight,
Where armies were slain, a most sickening sight.
With Grant to the Wilderness some went, as shown,
Where the field of the fray was with thousands strown.

Some one, too, of this Corps who was there can tell
How the gallant McPherson gore-covered fell.
In this company small, brave comrades there be
Who with Sherman fought, on his march to the sea.

You may class them as "bummers" or what you will,
It was brave men alone could their places fill.
And some were at Winchester too, on that day
When bold "Sheridan faced them the other way."

They have fought in the battles of Tennessee,
And their voices have shouted the victory.
In honoring them, we are honoring all
Our country's defenders, who came at her call.

They're ready if needed, each man tried and true,
To shoulder the musket, march forth in the blue.
As loyal to duty, to-day, as of yore.
Success to our comrades, The Veteran Corps.

THE PRISON-PEN.

INSCRIBED TO THE UNION EX-PRISONERS OF WAR.

BEYOND the years, down time's ravine,
Seems now to rise a fearful scene,
And, freezing all my veins anew,
That prison-pen is brought to view.
See, fifty thousand loyal men,
Languish and starve in prison-pen.

The wordless tale untold remains,
Of gnawing hunger, thirst, and pains.
Description fails, language affords
No aid; such suffering has no words.
Oh, sight unparalleled, I ken
Of fifty thousand prisoned men.

What torture rent the sufferer's frame
No art can paint, no language name:
Scant clothes had he to keep him warm;
No shelter from the sun or storm.
Each day he grew more faint, and then,
A lingering death in prison-pen.

Tempted each day his loyalty,
To join the foe and be set free—
Scorned the base terms, with courage high,
Dared to be loyal, or to die.
Oh, bravest were these patriot men
Thus racked in deadly prison-pen.

Such great temptations they withstood,
Sustaining life with loathsome food;
Obnoxious vapors filled the air;
A putrid stench had settled there.
Suffered and died in prison-pen,
Some fifty thousand Union men.

Of filth is formed the dank morass,
Through which each day the pris'ners pass.
They, gaunt and stiff, move but with groans,
While scurvy sores lay bare their bones—
Who can unfold the woes of men
Within this noisome prison-pen?

Not by the hand of soldier foe,
Who met and dealt them blow for blow;
They but the tools—by leaders see
Wrought out this great atrocity;
They, less than human, treated men
Worse than the brute in prison-pen.

A scanty piece of beef, so blue,
Alive with maggots wriggling through;
All green with mould, the scrap of bread,
On which the famished martyr fed,

Swallowed, perchance threw up again,
This poison dealt to prisoned men.

Hustled like beasts in rudest shed,
The crippled, dying, and the dead;
Shall they the name of surgeons give,
If such they had—who let them live?
Oh, men who rule! They knew not then,
They'd need this proof from prison-pen.

If o'er the dead-line crazed they go,
Are shot like beasts, in death laid low.
Try to escape—ah, fearful sound—
The baying of the fierce blood-hound,
Hunted, brought back, pray think you then
Words can describe this prison-pen?

The dead on wagons piled each day,
Like cords of wood, were hauled away;
In shallow trenches were they thrown,
Ere scarce the breath of life had flown.
Most sickening sight of prison-pen—
Worms crawl in flesh of living men.

In hosts who found release at last
Death's seeds were sown; they perished fast,
And memory limns that vacant stare,
Of men insane from suffering there.
And children cried at skeleton
With hungry eyes, like thing to shun.

May every year together bring
Comrades who shared that suffering.
The tales their memory might unfold
Can never in this world be told.
And, oh, rejoice that ne'er again
Shall brave men rot in prison-pen.

THE BATTLE OF CEDAR CREEK.

THE foes camped in each other's sight
By day discerned the smoke—at night
From camp to camp was seen the light
   Where hostile armies lay,
Until one morn at half-past three
Followed the sounding reveille,
Round after round of musketry;
   Began, the fierce affray.

The dull boom of artillery
   Mingles with battle-yells,
The blaze, the flash of musketry,
   The fiery, flying shells,
Screaming in winding, lurid curves:
'Neath galling fire our army swerves.

While battle-sound is roaring,
   Back to the camp retreat,
From steady fire outpouring—
   Confusion reigns complete;
The legions scatter, file and rank;
The foes our lines outflank!

But lo! the tide now turns,
Each heart with valor burns,
For Sheridan appears.
They welcome him with cheers.
He shouts, right merrily,
" Boys, face the other way."

Returning slowly, steadily,
   We make the foes retire,
When squadrons of our cavalry
   Charge on their ranks and fire,

Then onward sweeping, o'er the field
The routed enemy must yield.

Under that charge the rebels fled,
Leaving the dying and the dead.
Strewn with our soldiers' heavy loss,
The bloody battle-fields recross.
And thus, though lost, ere set of sun
Was Cedar Creek regained, rewon.

Within each nook in camp the dying,
The wounded, and the dead are lying,
  A thickly-fallen, patriot host,
And sadness marks each soldier's face
Who, mournful, notes each vacant place,
  In ranks and mess and picket post.

Their guns were ours, our guns regained,
Though peaceful quiet once more reigned,
  Our comrades we henceforth bewail,
Who there, with slaughtered thousands lay,
The bravest in the fierce affray,
  Who fell in Shenandoah's vale.

———————

OPEQUAN.

DEDICATORY TO LIEUTENANT-GENERAL PHILIP H. SHERIDAN.

Up came each brigade readily,
Though quick and silent, steadily,
The serried line moved gleamily—
  Thousands of men as one;
The leaders' chargers prancing,
The long blue line advancing;
A myriad bayonets glancing,
  Gleamed in the morning sun.

Forward! with courage flushing,
To charge of battle rushing,
Where falling shells are crushing,
　Forward! at double-quick.
Where war's dread cloud is lowering
From woods and rocks is roaring
The volleys outward pouring,
　And balls are flying thick.

Back! from this fire so galling,
Back! from the scene appalling,
Back! through your lines is falling
　In broken ranks, a host;
Yet two long weary hours,
'Neath leaden rain in showers,
Ye show your hero powers,
　Ye hold the fought-for post.

Till came the Eighth Corps in reserve,
Sturdy and fresh, with steady nerve,
Advancing lines that never swerve—
　All eager for the fray.
Then rang the soldiers' voices out,
In jubilant and joyful shout;
For soon the foe is put to rout—
　That hour decides the day.

Over the field our flag waves high;
There, where the dead and wounded lie,
Rises the long, long battle-cry—
　The foemen turn and run.
With fire, avenging, ye pursue,
Back to the town, then, driven through—
The scattered legions wildly flew.
　And thus the field was won.

Pursuing, with the coming morn,
With banners waving, scarred and torn,

Like veteran soldiers—battle worn—
  Whose hearts with duty thrill.
With skirmishing and driving in
The works, the weary hours begin.
For two long days—at length ye win
  The fight at Fisher's Hill.

At night ye climbed the mountain-side,
And crossed the chasms, deep and wide ;
At morn great numbers downward glide—
  In masses on them fall.
They turn, they fly in wild dismay—
Leave prisoners and artillery ;
For victory has closed the fray
  Beneath the mountain wall.

Forward bold Sheridan has led,
Leaving the wounded and the dead ;
Pursuing to the valley's head,
  Far up the blooming dell.
Your bayonets in the sunlight glance ;
Your lines form on the eminence ;
Your batteries eagerly advance,
  Swift hurling shot and shell.

Return again to Fisher's Hill ;
Attack the rear-guard with a will,
His ranks with consternation fill—
  The foe his fright reveals.
Ye drive them toward their infantry ;
Their baggage is your lawful prey ;
Ye capture their artillery,
  And "everything on wheels."

UNKNOWN.

A DECORATION ODE.*

WITH flowers we deck the soldiers' graves;
With drooping mast our standard waves,
Where flowers and lawn the dew-drop laves,
And breath of Spring is softly blown
O'er mounds where, on a simple stone,
The record says they were—Unknown.

With flowers, the brightest ones that bloom,
Be garlanded each soldier's tomb,
While sunbeams chase away the gloom.
Quell then the sigh, and still the moan,
Where head-post stands, like guardian lone,
Telling the oft-told tale—" Unknown."

---

* Recited by the author at Arlington National Cemetery, at the great tomb of the
" Unknown," Decoration Day, 1880, by special invitation from the Grand Army of the
Republic, Department of the Potomac.

Then cull the loveliest flow'rets bright,
And slowly walk, with footfall light,
Where sleep brave battlers for the right;
While sweeping breezes sob and moan,
Or zephyrs sigh in monotone
Like plaintive wail, for those Unknown.

Bring flowers and cast them thickly where
In leafy shade or sun's bright glare
The hillocks rise; pay tribute there;
There be your fairest chaplets thrown,
Though grass, unkempt and rankly grown,
Waves where no head-stone says—" Unknown."

Those head-boards o'er the hillocks fair—
We find them here and find them there;
We see them rising everywhere,
Standing like mourners, sad and lone,
Upon whose faces thought-lines shown
Form that one saddening word—Unknown.

From North to South, from East to West,
O'er all this land in freedom blest,
By breath of peace once more caressed,—
Full many a summer sun hath shone
Since Death his seed hath thickly sown,
With friend and foe, alike Unknown.

My father old, with pride uprose;
A patriot marched to meet the foes;
In Southern soil he found repose.
Dear loved one, whom I scarce had known,
My heart-thoughts be the flow'rets thrown,
To find thy grave, to me Unknown.

Two brothers growing side by side
In beardless youth, went, thrilled with pride.
In hospital one brother died.

I scarce can quell the rising moan ;
I seem to see him, ill and lone,
Dying, mid faces all Unknown.

That some hand scatter flowers, I pray,
O'er those I loved, who marched away
And came not back from day to day.
O'er all the land be flowers strown
Where sleep the brave, their faults condone,
Let strife and discord be Unknown.

Why do not flowers their fragrance shed
O'er heroes' graves, who fought and bled
In days of yore—our patriots dead ?
A century hath swiftly flown.
On history's page their deeds are shown ;
What though their names be all Unknown ?

Shoulder to shoulder, hand in hand,
They stood, a meagre, valiant band,
And nobly won a victory grand,
That brought us peace, and made our own
The fairest land on which e'er shone
Heaven's sunlight.   Are their graves Unknown ?

Then Germantown remember still,
And Brandywine, and Bunker Hill ;
While Trenton makes our bosoms thrill,
At Yorktown, Freedom's banner shone.
Oh, sacred dust of crumbling bone—
Erstwhile our sires, now all Unknown.

In this great tomb do myriads lie.
Let Fame unfurl their standard high—
Brave hearts whose glory was to die ;
Who, o'er the field, in forests lone,
Mingled the cheer with dying groan—
Myriads scarce numbered—all Unknown.

Thousands of hearts sad vigils keep;
Thousands of eyes with anguish weep,
Grieving for those who herein sleep.
Oh, sad hearts, know, by flowers strown,
A nation makes thy grief her own;
A nation mourns her dead Unknown.

Let grateful memories throng and rise;
Float fragrant incense to the skies;
Breathe, zephyrs, thy most tender sighs
Unceasingly, till time hath flown
And ages make this burial-stone
The hallowed shrine of those Unknown.

With flowery wreath shall all be crowned—
Sweet flowers of rhyme for every mound,
From Northern slope to Southern bound:
Rise harmony and monotone,
While sunbeams fall—sun-kisses thrown
With flowers of hope, for those Unknown.

In memory's garden long I sought
To cull the fairest flowers of thought,
A worthier tribute to have brought:
But the winged flowers, by zephyrs blown,
Soared upward to the great white throne,
For there the "Unknown" all are known.

THE SIEGE OF VICKSBURG.

At length ye view the lofty hills
Of Vicksburg. Every bosom thrills,
And every heart with courage high
Is nerved to dare, to do, or die.
The order brings them no alarm—
"At 10 A.M. the forts we storm."

Before the dawn, artillery crashes,
And flame of fire the city lashes;
Sulphurous smoke is hovering o'er;
With thundering peals the cannons roar;
The forts, reverberations shake,
While hills and waters rock and quake.

They ceased—one peal a signal ran—
At ten, the forward march began.
O'er hill and gulch swift hosts advance,
With faces stern and fearless glance,
Fighting for every inch of ground;
While comrades fall so thickly round.

They fell, mown down like blades of grass,
Or trees o'er which tornadoes pass.
Brave soldiers they, who would not yield
To foeman's sway, the bloody field;
Most harrowing, the havoc done—
The loss of life ere set of sun.

Soon, turning not to left nor right,
The General led from height to height;
The men pressed on; their battle-flag
Still proudly rose from crag to crag;
Till o'er the ramparts' wall they pour
A fire that stills the cannon's roar.

Here fell brave leaders, tried and true,
Here fell the patriot soldiers, too.
The slain lie thick o'er ridge and vale.
Repulsed, they yet again assail,
Till cloudy night they gladly greet,
Beneath whose shades the men retreat.

They leave the field, where yet remain
Three thousand wounded, maimed, and slain.
Soon tired out, on the ground they lay,
'Neath cooling rain, till dawn of day.

Sad duty; in the grassy dell,
Buried their comrades where they fell.

The armies grand, of General Grant,
A siege begin; new batteries plant,
And breastworks strong, more close advance,
Where thickly rebel bullets glance.
Not only shot and hurtling shell,
That broadcast o'er the city fell—

Were used, in deadly purpose for,
And priceless implements of war,—
But axe and barrow, pick and spade,
Roads opened and approaches made,
And trenches deep, and covered ways,
And earthworks thick and high they raise.

Closer and closer draws the line;
Fort after fort they undermine;
The fuse is lit—a thundering sound,
With trembling heaving of the ground;
Masses of earth rise and appall,
And, with huge timbers, backward fall.

On July Third a white flag waves
Upon the fort. The foeman craves
An armistice and interview,
To see what course he may pursue;
"Yield all," said Grant, without pretence,
"Or, sir, continue your defence."

On glorious Independence Day
Was victory won, through long delay;
High o'er the fort the standard rose,
O'er hundred thousands, friends and foes;
The Mississippi, grand and free,
Flowed once more, unvexed, to the sea.

Our banner o'er the Court-House floats,
Glad shouts uprise from myriad throats,

And once again "We'll rally round
The flag" is heard, triumphant sound,
Exultant, joyous pealings long,
And Vicksburg quivers with the song.

REUNION.

ONCE more in line, brave soldiers stand,
A scarred and maimed, and veteran band,
Grasping in fellowship each hand,
By link uniting all this land—
A link inured by battles dared,
More firmly joined by dangers shared.

Though years have flown more than a score,
Since clasped these hands in days of yore,
Call back those years, retread once more
Those battle-fields, those days live o'er,
Which memories to the mind restore,
Casting aside Time's misty screen,
Painting anew each thrilling scene,
O'er hill and gulch or deep ravine.

How starry eve, or morning sun,
More brightly shone on battles won;
When, Union colors planted here,
Ye rent the air with many a cheer.

That banner, then so proudly borne,
Shall never be of glory shorn,
Though faded, old, and sadly torn—
Symbol of veterans scarred and worn—
That veteran flag so proudly borne,
Leading you on, with drum and fife,
To save your country with your life.

Grief hides her face from History's lore
And weeping wails—"Returned no more."

That flag o'er this fair land must wave
Till nations sleep in freedom's grave;
That emblem led the true and brave,
And countless thousands freely gave
Their lives, its starry folds to save,
Who conquered armed hostility
That millions more might still be free.

My thoughts keep guard with measured tread
O'er silent bivouac of the dead—
O'er fields where friends and foes have bled—
O'er hospital or prison-bed—
O'er plains where Death his phalanx led.
My mind is as a lettered tome
In which is writ, " They ne'er came home."

Yet memory brings them back to me,
Who answer not the reveille;
Whose loving smiles I ne'er shall see;
Whose voice hear not—must ever be
Preserved by faithful memory.
Till trumpet-sound, on that great day,
Shall marshal all who marched away.

Greater than he who wears a crown,
Or purple robe or ermined gown—
Greater than he who wins renown,
Who with his arms his life lays down—
Aye, memory's torchlight brightly burns
For him who never more returns.
Now History, on her scroll of fame,
Enrols each hero's act and name;
Grief hides her face from History's lore
And weeping wails—" Returned no more."

Ah! many hearts are sad and lone,
Whose grieved refrain, an echoing tone,
Like muffled drum, hides stifled moan,
That else would be a throbbing groan.

Glory to them, each one and all,
Who answered to the nation's call!
Joy—you who meet, all battles o'er—
I wail, with Grief—"Returned no more!"

FURLOUGH.

Now home again our brave returning;
His heart with joy and valor burning
    As each loved scene appears.
Home! free from suffering, trials, danger,
Where he, alas, has been a stranger,
    For three long, weary years.

A brief respite with loved ones staying,
His country's voice again obeying,
    He goes to danger's toil.
How dear is home, how loved, how cherished,
When for that home he would have perished—
    Has battled for its soil.

BREAK RANKS.

A WINTER camp in Southern scene
Where waves a mass of gold and green,
    And then, no more to roam.
All battle-scarred the flag flung out,
Welcomed with heartfelt joyous shout,
    Our "Johnny comes marching home."

The rolling drums the heroes greet,
In grand review once more they meet;
    Receive the people's thanks,—
Display the dear, loved battle-flags,
Erst bright and new, now tattered rags,
    For last time here "Break ranks."

ONE FLAG, ONE COUNTRY.

CIVIL warfare, uncivilized carnage, is o'er.
Pray Heaven that brothers shall quarrel no more,
But clasp hands in friendship, though tears must be shed
With flowers that each spring-time are strown o'er the dead.

Yea, victor and vanquished have suffered and lost,
And victory gained was at terrible cost,
But the Union is saved and warfare is done,
And the nation is one, indissolubly one.

At Fredericksburg gather soldiers once more,
And former foes greet them, but not as of yore;
Where one army won, and one suffered defeat,
And thousands were slain, they in amity meet.

By cycles of years, father Time has concealed
The traces of war from the ensanguined field ;
Where carnage was thickest the tall grasses wave,
And swift limpid waters caressingly lave.

And here come the heroes from many a corps,
Approaching the battle scene, not as of yore ;
But with white-winged peace and with reverent tread,
The field, now the city of brave comrades, dead.

A motionless army lies silently here—
True heroes whose deeds are to memory dear.
A mission of love has the Veteran Corps,
With flowers, for memory, to cover them o'er.

MADRIGALS.

KINDRED THOUGHT.

SURELY Thought, that swiftly flies
Like a flash, must recognize
    Kindred Thought;
Else, on earth were void and vain
All the pleasure; all the pain
    Borne for naught.

And the poet—mission grand—
Giveth us to understand
    This belief.
Fraught with sympathy and cheer
Are his flowing lines, sincere,
    Page and leaf.

A METAPHOR.

As the Sun down reaches to drink the sea
    And the sea uplifts to the Sun,
Thus doth my lover bend down to me
    As I lift my lips to his own.

ALL FAIR THINGS MUST PERISH.

ALAS, that all fair things must perish!
    They gladden the sight, and decay.
Alas, that the bright hopes we cherish,
    Beam on us, then hasten away!

A VALENTINE.

WHAT may I send for a valentine
But tender thoughts from my heart to thine;
With hope that the token may please thee well?
Its wealth of affection no words can tell.

THE ORATOR.

ONE of the few, who well, and truly scan
The author's lines, the hidden thoughts to find,
Traced by the silent-moving pen; and can
Interpret pathos, passion, tenderness;
Their depth of joy or grief impress
By human tones, upon the list'ner's mind.

JOSEPHINE.

FOR kindly thought doth glow upon her face;
Her eyes proclaim the wistful loving soul,
And picture forth a gentle spirit's grace,
And this it is that makes her beautiful.

A FRAGMENT.

To be, to do, and to suffer;
These words do tell—
(I have conned them well)
Our lot on earth.
I live, I exist;
Of the work to be done,
I do what I can,
And believe me, dear friend,
I suffer.

THE POET-SOUL.

THE tender sigh, the plaintive moan,
Are not for Poet-souls alone;
But yearning longings, unexpressed,
Lie trembling in the Poet's breast,
Breathing the sad, yet thrilling strain
Of ecstasy's exquisite pain.

LOVE'S ILLUSION.*

I FANCIED he kissed me on lips and on brow.
So light the caress, yet it thrilleth me now;
And shall I confess, without favor, or fear?
He became from that hour, from that moment, more dear.
But alas! may my frankness not frowardness seem,
For he never has kissed me—'twas only a dream.

HOPELESS LOVE.

'TIS true you love no more, while I,
Waken to know that love can die—
Waken to know that hath been given,
To bring regret, a taste of Heaven;
Live but to know the fond caress
Was all of earthly happiness;
Live but to feel the longing pain
Of hopeless love—unloved again.

IMPROMPTU.

My thoughts are little singing birds,
    That ever fly to thee;
If I their carols put in words,
    'Tis thus I set them free.
If thy heart-thoughts are other birds
    That struggle to be free,
Unloose their pinions, give them words,
    And let them fly to me.

NATURE'S NOBLEMAN.

A FALSE aristocrat is he
Whose fame depends on ancestry,
Or wealth to purchase high degree—
Far nobler men of humbler birth;
Start from the lowlier ranks of earth;
Hew their own path, and prove the worth
Of labor's aristocracy.

---

* Published in sheet-music form by John Church & Co., Cincinnati.

LOVE'S ROUNDELAY.*

An ecstatic thrill expresses
Not the measure of the blisses
Folded in her fond caresses;
E'en in dreams I feel her kisses;
Equal rapture she confesses,
As my heart with love she blesses;
As her lips to mine she presses.

INVOCATION TO LOVE.

O Love, thy praises, long have I,
  In poet's rhythm sung;
My thoughts, like fays, around thee fly
  Like pearls, are o'er thee flung.
Flood with thy sunshine, now, my sky,
  Where erst dark clouds have hung;
So shall my heart discard the sigh,
  My harp, for joy, be strung.

HEAVEN.

Confronted oft with care,
  Or threatening woe appalling,
We gaze with face affrighted—
Our fairest dreams then blighted—
  To Heaven, our spirit calling,
Would take its flight, up there.

FOR THY FAIR FLOWERS.

For thy fair flowers, fraught with fragrance rare,
  To crown the effort, heart and mind had made,
Receive in lieu my sprays of thought, less fair,
Since flowers from fancy's realm may not compare
  With nature's bloom, yet they less quickly fade.

---

* Susceptible of transposition of lines without disturbing the continuity of thought or grammatical structure.

MAY.

A GOLDEN buttercup thou gavest me,
The first that greeted thee in early spring;
I folded in my note-book leaves, the spray;
A gladsome opening bud; 'twas like to thee.
Three years have swiftly passed. Again to-day
It meets once more mine eye, the while I pray
That thou too gladden, like this fairy thing—
To many loving hearts, thy presence bring
A joyous happiness, with its fair bloom,
And drive from weary lives dull care away;
With thy soul's beauty oft dispelling gloom,
Thy life mature to perfect blossoming.

ALL OTHER LOVES ABOVE.

I LOVE you, yet I know not why,
Nor wherefore, only know that I
    Do love you truly, love you well,
All other loves above.
So well my love, I love,
    Nor pen nor tongue can tell.

BLISS SUPREME.

THERE's bliss supreme,
In love's bright beam,
That glistens through a tear.

THE STATUE.

I STAND on a base of common sense—
A pedestal firm with which to commence.
A bud of Genius is in my hand,
To bloom, perhaps, in a better land.
My brow is crowned with flowers of love—
A priceless gift from Heaven above;
But, ah! their fragrance makes me human;
I wake, I weep, I am—a woman.

HOPES AND FEARS.

We find, as we traverse life's paths, through the years,
Our hopes are as sunbeams, as shadows our fears.

WOMAN TRUE AND BEAUTIFUL.

The blessings woman's love hath brought,
The imagery her fancy caught,
The work of art her genius wrought,
The priceless wealth of woman's thought,
From mind and heart all beauty fraught,
And form of grace, have artists sought
To picture forth, with noble soul,
Of woman true, and beautiful.

A FLORAL OFFERING.

Fair flowers their perfume most potent distil,
And touch all my senses with ecstasy's thrill;
And the love that bestowed them, though blossoms may die,
Like a vision, in memory lingers for aye.

EXCUSE FOR LYRICS.

I sing of love and kindred themes
   'Tis true, and wherefore should I not?
Love smiles upon our brightest dreams,
   And sits enthroned in every spot,
Where dwelleth joy. In Heaven above,
Love reigns, for God himself, is love.

FOR, IF WE STRIVE.

For, if we strive to do the right,
Or seek to make some pathway bright—
Strengthen some heart, or soothe some pain,
We shall not, then, have lived in vain.

THE HUMAN MIND.

How strange, incomprehensible, the human mind!
Its scope how vast, and yet how undefined!

LOVE'S GIFT.

IF I, like love, the clouds might rift,
  O'er poesy's hidden shrine;
I'd kneel in her presence, her veil uplift;
  Ah! henceforth forever she's mine,
    She is mine!
Henceforth and forever she's mine!
For poesy ever is love's purest gift,
    Precious gift:
And yet, like these lines, she is thine;
  Love's gift, truly thine.

A HEART THAT E'ER THROBS WITH EMOTION.

DID ever one love thee more truly,
More sweetly, more fondly, more fully,
  With self-abnegation complete?
A pearl from the depth of the ocean,
A heart that e'er throbs with emotion,
  Is the gift that I lay at thy feet.

WOMAN'S ENFRANCHISEMENT.

FOR sophistry must float away,
Like vapor clouds 'neath light of day;
And Right, and Justice, ope the way,
To woman's full enfranchisement.

THOUGHTS OF ME.

As in this floral vine, in thee,
May grace and sweetness both combine;
And, like its tendrils, still may twine
Around thy heart, some thoughts of me.

SABLE-WINGED HOURS.

THE sable-winged hours,
Like shadows of night,
Brood over the spirit
And darken its light.

MUSIC'S SAD REFRAIN.

OFT, joy, and love, and sorrow's silent depth of pain,
Are given full expression, in music's sad refrain.

MAIDEN LOVELINESS.

As rosebud on the parent stem,
　　Thus is a maiden's loveliness ;
As pure and fair as pearly gem,
　　With priceless love to cheer and bless.

THE SOURCE OF WISDOM.

HE who hath strayed, with joy, through realms of thought,
Charmed by the beauties sportive fancy caught ;
Revelled in scenes by bounteous Nature wrought,
And felt the bliss imagination brought ;
To him hath inspiration's magic taught
The source of wisdom, else so vainly sought.

WERE LOVE BUT A THEME.

WERE love but a mythical, fanciful theme,
But a flickering sunbeam of golden gleam,
But the mystical fount of a shadowy stream,
A vanishing vision, a beautiful dream,
How, then, could love crown us with bliss so supreme ?

WOMAN'S IDEAL.

OF fair, commanding presence, yet no whit austere ;
A man to love, to honor, and to (slightly) fear ;
Whose lips are eloquent, whose wondrous, speaking eyes,
Express the noble thoughts that through their depth arise.

THE POET'S SAD SONG.

A GRIEVED and resistless throbbing
　　Is heard in the poet's sad song,
As sea-waves, surging and sobbing,
　　The billows are bearing along.

A PRAYER.

Yes, pray God give me "brain to think,"
At wisdom's fountain let me drink.
Pray God to give me "heart to feel,"
And on that heart impress His seal;
To purer air on "wings to soar,"
Until I reach the heavenly shore.
Pray, too, He give me "voice to sing,"
To voiceless love expression bring.

COMPENSATION.

And he, on earth, who trials great endureth,
    That try the strength, yet elevate the soul,
Still struggles on, life's barque in safety mooreth,
    And casts its anchor in the heavenly goal.

EXPERIENCE.

By the light of experience, we gather
    The truths we had doubted for years,
That the bright rippling streamlet of laughter
    Has source in the fountain of tears.

THE RIVER OF LIFE.

In the river of life bitter tear-drops of woe
    Make yet purer the fount, more pellucid its flow.
Sorrow cleanseth the heart, and refresheth like dew,
    Makes translucent the thought, as air blended in snow.

WINGÈD MILE-POSTS.

As the years of thy life all unheeded fly past,
May these wingèd mile-posts, e'en to the last,
Be numbered with joys, all unshaded with care,
And each passing year be more bright and more fair,
May bright evergreen memories cling round thy heart,
Buds of promise and love of life's wreath, form a part,
With sweet thoughts intertwined, is the wish I may bring,
And a Hawthorn (Hope's blossom) my verse-offering.

WHISPERINGS LOW.

SPIRIT breathings like whisperings low
 Sendeth my spirit to thine,
 Freighted with wishes divine,
That never another may feel, or know
 The longing and yearning of mine.

MOTHER-LOVE.

MY darling child, when time shall send
 To thee, the friendship, love of others,
Whose lives, whose thoughts with thine shall blend,
 Thou'lt find no love more true than—mother's.

FLOWERS OF THOUGHT.

'TIS wintry weather now; the flowers
 Are only flowers of thought I send.
They may beguile some weary hours
 And sometimes bring to mind your friend.

LIFE A DREAM.

LIFE is a dream that flits away;
 Love an ethereal vapor, blown
By winds of fate, or zephyrs' play,
 Gone almost ere in fulness known.

SUCH LOVE IS PURE.

LOVE as ye love the flowers that bloom
To please with beauty and perfume.
Love as ye would the good and wise.
Such love is pure; such love we prize.

PAINFUL BLISS.

THE trembling yearning of a soul
That longs to reach a peaceful goal;
The painful bliss that thrills a heart
Till transports cause the tears to start.

17

RAPTUROUS LOVE.

My heart sings like the starling,
 Air-swung in leafy grove;
To tender words, my darling,
 It thrills with rapturous love.

HOPE'S STAR.

Hope's star shines forth, a beacon-light
 Through stormy clouds of sorrow,
And presages a pathway bright
 Where sun-beams smile to-morrow.

LIBERTY.

O'er this broad land from main to main
 Throughout the western world,
O'er oceans wide, o'er mount and plain,
 Her standard floats unfurled.

GOD IS LOVE.

The zephyr whispers of His soothing care;
He lifts my spirit on the wings of prayer;
He teaches me, in all things bright and fair,
That He is Love, and "Love is everywhere."

THE RECOMPENSE OF JOY.

As 'prisoned bird, whose plaintive singing
 May thrill the heart with joyous glow,
Thus happiness to others bringing,
 Hath recompense who would forego?

POESY'S FLOWERS.

When fancy o'er my mind held sway,
 There poesy's flowers grew,
And now I bring a little spray,
While in this page you sure may find
A vine, wherewith the flowers to bind;
 'Tis kindly thought for you.

THY PICTURED FACE.

I GAZE upon thy pictured face,
In eyes serene as skies above,
Wherein appears a spirit's grace
And wondrous wealth of woman's love.

LOVE'S SWEET PASSION.

LOVE's sweet passion thrills me, fills me
With a trembling, strange desire,
Through my being flowing, glowing,
As a bright, ecstatic fire.
Yet its light still warms me, charms me
With an ecstasy divine;
Nor its glow alarms, nor harms me.
Glad am I love's thrill is mine.

A SCION OF OLD ROYALTY.*

GREAT healer, of whose wondrous skill
Cured patients are expatiating,
'Tis plain to see that you must be
A knight of very high degree—
A scion of old royalty;
Since, at your call, 'tis proved, you will
Keep full a score of " maids in waiting."

MY CHILD'S REQUEST.

MYLA came but yesterday,
Pleading, to me, from her play;
And, "Mamma, I wish," said she,
"You would write a verse for me."
Could I then that wish refuse?
Called I to my aid, the muse;
Bring I, darling, now, with this,
Mother-love and birthday kiss.

---

* Written while waiting with a score of ladies in the reception-room to consult a physician.

THE WOODBINE'S BECKONING FINGERS.

Round this dear haunt my fancy lingers
And hovers near the graceful vine,
Whose leaflets sway like beckoning fingers,
Whose tendrils, like heart-thoughts, entwine.

TO ADA.

A loving token I would send
To thee, my winsome, fair, young friend,
I'd search through fancy's brightest bowers
And cull for thee thought's wingèd flowers.
Like birds on airy pinions, they
Should float, to bless, with joy, thy day;
Bearing my prayers and hopes for thee,
In thy sad hours, my sympathy.

A HOPE.

May never clouds of sorrow o'er thee blend,
Whom now I greet on this auspicious day.
May He who watches o'er us, kindly send
Thee many peaceful, happy ones, I pray.
May, like a pure and radiant gem of light,
A guiding star, thy life forever be;
Until thy spirit takes its heavenward flight,
Thy soul puts on the robe of immortality.

DOES YOUR HEART KEEP CALLING?

Does your heart keep calling me, darling
As mine is calling to you,
Through a pure sweet depth of tenderness
That proveth love holy and true?

A SOURCE OF JOY.

Be it thine, dear one, to choose the wiser part,
Thy mind with knowledge store, with tenderness thy heart.
In realms of truth and love find peace without alloy,
And own a lasting pleasure in thine inner source of joy.

DEAR, GENTLE GIRL.

Dear, gentle girl, left motherless,
  Ere scarce of womanhood aware,
To soothe the younger child's distress,
  To smooth thy father's brow from care.
Dear, gentle girl, my wish for thee,
  Words are but powerless to express;
May joy and love unceasingly
  Be thine, thy life on earth to bless.

IN POET'S PHRASE.

To woman's love, or woman's joy, or woman's bitter grief,
Expression given in poet's phrase, will sometimes bring relief.

ANNETTE.

Now what shall I say to thee, Annette,
Annette my darling, Annette my pet?
Shall I speak of the azury depth of thine eyes,
(May never a tear to their fair surface rise!)
Of thy cheeks like the rose,
Of that *retrousse* nose,
Or the half-hidden beauties thy dimples disclose?
Nay, nay, I tell thee, I'll write no such stuff,
I say but, "I love thee." Is that not enough?
But that thou art handsome, my last line will prove—
We see every beauty in those whom we love.

MY SISTER.

Dear Hattie, sister of my heart,
  With spirit blithe and free;
And nature void of every art,
  Thou'rt beautiful to me.
I pray that Heaven may bless thy life
  And years may bring to thee,
As sister, daughter, maid, or wife,
  A happy destiny.

THE FORGET-ME-NOT.

IN future years, in many a weary hour,
  When I may dwell in some far distant spot,
My heart would then, e'en like this little flower
  In its dear name, bid thee " forget me not."

EPIGRAM TO IDA MORE.

THE time will come, full soon to pass,
  When thou wilt be no more, alas!
And yet may health and golden store
  Be thine when thou'rt a lass no More.

MAY THY FAIR LIFE.

MAY thy fair life be as a day of gladness
  Whose bright hours pass unshaded by a care,
Unfraught with pain, undimmed by cloud of sadness—
  Thus breathes o'er thee the spirit of my prayer.

MY FRIEND.

LIKE a full blooming rose thou art,
  Dear Sister and Mother and Wife,
Noble thoughts and sweet love in thy heart
  Are rounding, in beauty, thy life.

THE MASTER OF ART.

THOUGH his sketches, like grand panegyric,
  With emotion must touch every heart;
Swaying hearts in a manner empiric,
  Yet he knows but one love—love of art.

CRITIC'S SOPHISTRY.

IT were the merest sophistry
  For critic to depose
That only fools write poetry,
  While genius sticks to prose.

LASTING TREASURE.

THOUGHT, I hold, is lasting treasure ;
Joy has wings and soon will fly.
When the soul is thrilled with pleasure
Springs the tear-drop to the eye.

More than wealth or high position ;
Worldly dross—who can compare
With that higher, holier mission,
Breathed in poet's song of prayer ?

FANCY'S FLOWERS MEET THE CRITIC'S EYE.

I GATHERED sweet wild flowers, that grew along my way,
Because they gave me pleasure, each cherished, little spray ;
Nor did I dream, the posies, that grew 'neath nature's sky,
The blossoms of the wayside, would meet the florist's eye,
Who may pronounce them worthless, and bid me cast aside
The modest clustered garland, that was erstwhile my pride.
And thus my flowers of fancy may meet the critic's eye,
Before whose chilling glances, they fall and fade and die.

ACROSTICS.

MARIE.

Merry hearted dainty maiden,
And as fair as dream of Aiden—
Radiant are thine eyes, and tender;
In their depths a starlike splendor
Ever beams—the light of love.

Rich thou art, for love enthralls thee,
On thee waits,—no ill befalls thee;
Utmost care folds thee from harm,
Nursling of fond hearts the charm—
Dainty Spirit from above
Sent to hallow earthly love.

MYLA.

My darling girl, could you believe
Yourself displaced by any other?
Loved one, you make my spirit grieve,
And yet none are so dear to—mother.

MINNIE.

May happiness pervade thy life
In all pursuits thy steps attend,
Nor hand of sorrow, toil, or strife,
Nor stroke of grief, their burdens lend
In every deed be true and kind;
Ennobling joys thou thus shalt find.

Merry hearted, dainty maiden,
And as fair as dream of Aidenn.

GERTRUDE.

GREAT love as bright as sunlight's beam
E'er bless thy life with joy supreme.
Right royal are the gifts, I ween,
That Nature gives to sweet sixteen.
Rich are thy clustered beauties now;
Unmarred by care thy placid brow;
Deep are thine eyes of lustrous hue,
Enshrining soul-light, beaming through.

CHARLOTTE.

CHARLOTTE, the joyous household pet,
Hovered about with restless feet;
A wee bright maiden, scarcely yet
Released from mother's span, so sweet,
Love's dearest circlet, mother's arms.
O'er all the rest my heart had sought her—
Took she my fancy by her charms—
Then flowed her words like running water;—
" Ever so much I love—your daughter."

ANNA.

A SWEET voice echoes in my ear,
Now write a poem, for me, here;
Nor would I those bright eyes refuse—
A poem? yes! Pray fetch my muse.

MERTIE.

MY girl friend, striving to excel,
Each heritage of Hope be thine;
Right thoughts, high aims, in thee combine:
Truth beautiful e'er with thee dwell.
If wish of mine prevailed, each sun,
Each hour should score thy laurels won.

ALICE.

ALL soulful are her eyes of blue,
Low voiced the music from sweet lips,
Inwreathed with smiles that oft pursue,
Chasing the dimples they eclipse:
Each speaking feature proves her true.

HATTIE.

HERE in this book I write my name
And try to smuggle in another,
That they who read perhaps the same,
Therein find sister, friend, or brother;
Indeed, to learn who's dear to me,
Each one who reads her name may see.

HELEN.

HEREWITH, dear friend, I send a thought,
E'en swiftest bird that soareth free;
Love's message in its pinions wrought;
Else other eyes than thine, would see,
'Neath wing of thought, my love for thee.

HAIL, JULY FOURTH.

HAIL, glorious morn of Freedom's birth!
A nation's day of gladsome mirth
Inspires her sons with loyalty;
Liberty is her royalty.
Joy brings the brightest hours of glee
Upon this anniversary.
Loud booms the gun, glad chimes the bell,
Youth celebrates no day so well.
Folds of the starry flag float free—
Our standard waves from sea to sea.
Upon the soil by patriots won,—
Rejoicings rule, joy, mirth, and fun.
Time that computes the centuries
Hath ne'er a day to rank with this.

INDEX.

267

THE END.

719